TH

AND THE
OLD DRAGON

N T Layne

THE YOUNG KNIGHT
AND THE
OLD DRAGON

N. T. LAZER

www.ntlazer.com

ISBN-13: 978-1-7355616-2-2

The Gratoa
Sea

Kolog
Bay

The
Western
Range

Kolog

Banti

Kit

Vesta
Cave

Vesta
Forest

Pallas

Merdo

Sekoa

Deserted Desert

Torn
Bay

Torn

Dosdo

Rork

Stanvs

Arlo

Ro

Berdvn

Rowa Lake

Dervin

01

Flames danced before the amassed crowd of people. They wiggled and lept from tree to tree, lighting the way for more tendrils of flames to lick the next piece of flora and consume it mercilessly. Like a snowfall, the smoke from the ruined trees rose high and lazily floated down to the village ahead. The crowd watched in amazement, entranced by the dazzling display of destruction.

All were in awe except for one.

Aten the Knight stood a few paces beyond the crowd. Just a few moments ago he had felt a rush of success flowing through him. Though young, Aten had recently earned the title of Dragonslayer after defeating the Great Slayer of Armies: Vesta the Dragon. From the endeavor, he suffered major wounds to his shoulder and calf. And although he had succeeded in slaying Vesta, Aten had a knot in his stomach, feeling much worse now than he did in the morning when Vesta was alive. It was all due to a shrilling yell he heard far off in the forest shortly after Vesta's death. Vesta's father—also a dragon—had discovered her body, and was determined to know her killer's name.

"My good people of Pallas," Aten called to the onlookers gripped by wonder, "why do you watch the forest so passively? We must flee this place at once!"

"Flee? I have never seen a dragon's death throes before. It is fascinating," Elder Anderson, the village leader, said, his eyes glittering with fascination and tears. For some strange reason, Aten believed he sounded defensive.

"Death throes!?" Aten said, limping forward on his good leg.

"Yes, the struggle that the body bears before the soul leaves it. Humans are so morbid to watch, but the dragon seems to have brought about an explosion of flames! There is no need to leave," Anderson said. The forest branches snapped thunderously.

"Elder Anderson, the dragon who resided in the cave is dead. There are no throes to be had. This is not her doing, this is a greater evil," Aten said quietly once he stood in front of him. "Tell the people to flee. They will listen to you."

Anderson still watched the fiery scene beyond Aten, his face glowing a harsh orange tinge.

"You say that you killed the dragon, but you do not know what one looks like dead. Perhaps their bodies perish in flames. Besides, what evil could create this other than the dying dragon?" Anderson asked. Aten felt uncomfortable speaking so casually about the death of Vesta.

"Another dragon!" Aten urged, still quiet enough as not to cause widespread panic to the people of Pallas.

"Another dragon? This dragon came from nowhere and demands we leave?" Anderson said with a snort. "Of all the creatures, why would you suppose *another* dragon exists?"

"Did you not hear the distressed cry asking who killed his daughter?" Aten asked incredulously.

"You assume that was a dragon? For it is impossible that any man could be in the forest of a dragon discovering that his daughter had been killed by it while out of his sight?" Anderson asked agitatedly. "Aten, this is a victory. You are a Dragonslayer now! A title that has gone unearned, even during my lifetime! Can you not let your anxieties abate for one moment and realize what peace you have brought on this land?"

"This is not peace!" Aten said, stabbing a finger toward the burning trees. "This is a declaration of war from a dragon!" Aten yelled. A few worried glances turned his way. He did nothing to assuage them.

"Aten, watch your tongue, there are worried people among us," Anderson scolded.

"People who will die if we do nothing!" Aten said, his voice rising further. More heads turned his way. Aten caught eyes with a few knights from his guild.

"Brothers!" he called, waving them toward him with his good arm. They made their way, Boros at the lead.

"Aten," Anderson warned.

"We must flee the village!" Aten urged the knights.

"What? Why, did you not defeat the dragon?" Boros asked, surprised.

"Aten believes there to be a dragon headed in our direction at this very moment," Anderson said, waving an arm flippantly.

"That is right!" Aten said hurriedly, happy to see Anderson coming to reason.

"And I seem to remember the guild told me he swore a solemn oath that he would not return unless a dragon no longer burdened our town," Anderson said. Aten's jaw dropped as he stared at Anderson, shadows floundering on his fuming face.

"Is this true?" Boros said, taking hold of his sword. He was honor-bound to kill Aten if he returned without having fulfilled his oath.

"I—y—no, I…" Aten looked between Boros and Anderson, his head swimming with confusion.

"Aten, there is no need to panic. It is fine," Anderson said with a soothing voice. "Either it is the case that what we are witnessing are the death throes of a dragon that you have slain, or you seem to believe that against all odds another dragon has come to displace us from this beautiful village of Pallas over which we have resided for generations."

Aten could not believe what he was hearing. He had never seen Anderson speak with such malice before. He tried to understand where it was coming from. As a tree crashed to the forest floor behind him, he began to wonder why the village elder would act so irrationally. Was he set in his ways? Or was this anger of a jealous nature? Was he afraid to leave the village? He had so little to fear when he was treated as the village leader.

"Well, Aten, do you believe there is a dragon coming or not?" the elder asked, eyebrows raised impatiently.

Aten's eyes darted around his guild members for looks of comradery, but all he saw was confusion and fear. He shook his head.

"I suggest we flee, regardless of the circumstances. The flames could reach—"

"The flames are a great distance from the village, we are at a perfect place to enjoy the display," Anderson said, happily.

"I..." Aten's eyes stung with tears of frustration. "Anderson, why is it that you are afraid to leave Pallas when it is in danger?"

"I am not afraid to leave Pallas!" Anderson said, arms opening wide, "I *am* afraid of listening to a boy tell the village to leave its home to some other forsaken land and living by their rules because of a *feeling* he has about a dragon that he just killed!"

Boros and the other knights looked to Anderson with surprise, joining Aten in experiencing the first time Anderson was acting out of character. Aten wiped the spittle off of his face, taking note of the words Anderson said.

"You fear to lose your power over the lives of the people of Pallas," Aten spoke as he came to the realization.

"What!?" Anderson said, his face growing darker.

"You want to remain because at least you have control here as the elder. Elsewhere they may have different rules that would render you powerless. Pallas is the only place you can maintain superiority," Aten said, the flames cracking behind him seemingly in agreement. Boros looked nervously between the two of them. Anderson's face flickered in the flamelight, his eyes seething.

"Very well. We will play your way," Anderson spat, his teeth gritted tightly. He turned to Boros and the knights, "Kill him for failure to meet his oath."

02

Boros's eyes went wide as his eyebrows furled downward.

"You want us to kill him?" Boros clarified. He was looking into the blaze now as if searching for the dragon within it.

"Anderson be reasonable!" Aten shouted, though in his heart he knew they had the right to carry out his punishment for the failure of holding to his oath.

"Was I unclear?" Anderson hissed, ignoring Aten, "He was once allied with the dragon and now he has brought it to us!" He pointed a wrinkled finger to the forest but kept his steely gaze on Aten.

"Well then there is only one thing to do," Boros said, breathing in deeply and winking at Aten.

"Evacuate!!" Boros screamed, turning to the crowd and waving his sword to grab their attention. "Gather whatever belongings you need for immediate travel and evacuate Pallas! We have it on Anderson's good word that we are in danger!"

"What!?" Anderson exclaimed, shifting his animosity to Boros in the span of one syllable.

"You said it yourself!" Boros said loud enough to keep the villagers listening, "You believe that a dragon has been brought to us!"

"By Aten!" Anderson yelled.

"And it was by Aten that we were informed of this!" Boros nodded. Aten watched him with awe, the confidence he exuded carrying itself into every word he spoke. The villagers looked to one another worried, then quickly began to disperse, scurrying away from the fiery view to gather what they could from their homes. Anderson pulled Boros by the neck plate in his armor.

"What are you doing!?" he hissed. "Kill him and call back the people! We don't want to panic them!"

"I am only keeping my word to protect the people! You said there was a dragon!" Boros said facetiously.

"Yes, but—nevermind, kill the boy and we will discuss the matter more thoroughly," Anderson said, trying to throw Boros Aten's way. Boros remained rigid in place.

"Kill my guild brother? On what grounds?" Boros said. Aten peered at him, unable to read what he was saying. Even the knights behind Boros seemed confused but eager to follow his lead to not killing Aten.

"He swore that he would not return unless there was no dragon burdening this town. Now there is a dragon coming down on us! What more do you need!?" Anderson roared at him.

"Dragon? I do not see any dragon!" Boros said, standing on his toes in a display of looking into the flames. "And you said yourself that the flames were a safe distance from the town, so there is no burden I can see coming from this. I think it would be safe to say that we should not carry out our word unless we determine without a doubt that a dragon is coming."

"Then why did you tell the villagers to flee!?" Anderson's face had gone completely red, blending in with the shades of light coming from the forest fire.

"I thought it prudent to take proper precautions based on the word of my village leader. Even if excessive, it would be smart just to keep our people safe," Boros said. Anderson huffed, then looked at Aten up and down. Aten felt naked without any weapon and knew Anderson was sizing him up.

"Fine, I will kill him myself," Anderson said, drawing the sword from an unsuspecting knight. Boros caught his arm and gripped it tightly.

"I cannot let you harm a guild brother. He is sworn to protect the people and the town, same as I. It would be absurd to kill them for no reason," Boros said. Anderson tried to shake away his grip.

"For no reason? He broke an oath—"

"He made an oath to the guild, not to anyone else. We are the only ones who may dole out his punishment. Now I suggest you evacuate with the rest of our contingent," Boros said, swinging Anderson around and pushing his back toward the village. Anderson stared with wide eyes, then threw the sword to the floor, enraged.

"I will return to the village, but I will not leave! There is no danger coming and I will be certain to tell others not to leave as well," Anderson screamed, stomping away.

"I may have made a powerful enemy," Boros said, to the knight closest to him. The knight chuckled. Aten licked his lips, trying to think of something to say.

"Boros, I—"

"Say nothing Aten. We must assist the villagers in escaping whatever threat is coming immediately. Then you must explain yourself to us and we will determine the true fate of your oath," Boros said.

03

The knights of the guild ran from home to home, collecting belongings of men, women, and children to flee the village of Pallas as fast as they could muster. Most families were quick to comply, the fire looking more foreboding the more time they took to gather items. Everyone was headed to the Hills of Ramos in the Northeast, a location that would have a clear view of the village and forest from afar.

"Ren, you grab anyone left in the Hessertonia household," Boros commanded. "Aten, you go to Waron's forge and make sure he has already evacuated. Help him with anything you can, but ensure he does not carry more than is reasonable."

"Right," Aten nodded, hobbling toward the forge with his bad leg.

"And be sure to check on his neighbors as well!" Boros called, running ahead to the next house.

"Waron!" Aten yelled as he approached. He saw that the blacksmith's neighbor's chimney stack was billowing and wondered what could be burning at this time. "Waron, are you there?"

Aten began to bang on the door. He turned his face to the blazing forest once more, noting more smoke and ash than fire, but still no sign of Vesta's father. He heard the clink of metal inside and prepared to ram the door. He breathed in deeply and charged, throwing the force of his weight into the collision. Smashing into the door sent a searing pain down his arm and caused him to cry out in pain. Already, he had forgotten about the wound in his shoulder and likely exacerbated its damage. He reached up with his good arm and turned the door handle.

Apparently, it had been unlocked the entire time.

He pulled the door open and clamored inside.

"Waron!?"

"Aten!" Waron called from the other side of the room, gazing at a wall of weapons. He waved him over with one hand while the other scratched his chin.

"Waron, why haven't you evacuated yet?"

"I cannot determine which weapons are best to take on my cart," he said, pointing his small metal cart with a thumb. It was piled high with nothing but armors, shields, bows, and arrows.

"What—what about food? Or anything other than metal goods?" Aten asked, getting a closer look at the cart.

"I will not need them. Once we are out there, people will want meat. Their supplies will run low and they will come to me for materials in exchange for anything I desire," Waron said with a grand smile.

"Do not be foolish Waron, pack some food and clothing!" Aten protested.

"I have all the weaponry I will need to exchange for that," he said, picking up a spear, weighing it and adding it to his pile. He looked over to Aten who was lost in thought, trying to think of points to convince Waron to be more pragmatic.

"For example," Waron said, pointing at Aten's hip, "you are lacking a sword. I will sell you one in exchange for dragging the cart up the hill for me. That way I have more room to carry more swords!"

Aten looked to his injured leg and sighed. He needed the sword more than he needed comfort.

"Fine," Aten said.

"Excellent!" Waron said, looking at Aten while tilting his head. He picked up a sword and threw it to Aten. Aten ducked out of the way, allowing it to clatter to the floor.

"Not how I would have imagined you would take the sword, but it is yours to abuse, I suppose," he said, looking back to the remaining weapons on the wall. Aten picked up the sword and balanced it in his hand. He was not surprised by how comfortable he was with it. Waron was good at his craft despite how aloof he acted. He sheathed the blade and went to pull the cart. It was surprisingly heavy and took his full weight to drag it behind him. Even pulling it to the front door put him under great strain.

"I will meet you at the hill. I must first check on your neighbor." Aten breathed, deciding whether he regretted the decision now or would leave the regret for later.

"Yes, yes," Waron nodded, picking up another spear and weighing it.

Aten walked out of the forge and limped to the neighbor with the inactive chimney. After trying to open the door first, he attempted to knock then called inside. It seemed no one was home. Satisfied, he went to the other neighbor and knocked loudly.

"Who is it?" called a slow, gruff voice from inside, "Waron? I told ya I do not want ta buy any of ya weapons!"

"No, this is the Knight Aten, assisting with the evacuation!" Aten called back in. He bounced in place impatiently. The man sounded like he was in no hurry.

"Ah, a knight, eh? Not interested."

"Not...interested?" Aten asked, dumbfounded.

"That is right," the man said.

Aten wrung his hands, confused.

"We are evacuating the village. To safety?" Aten said, unsure of why the man was acting so casual.

"I am well aware of what tha village is up ta. Not interested," he said plainly.

"But you are in danger!" Aten yelled, pounding on the door.

"Oh yes, I am aware of tha danger of ya bandits stealing my possessions once ya clear out tha village, eh?"

"Band—No, I am trying to protect you from the incoming dragon—"

"Oh yes, the *dragon*. I never heard of a dragon for all the years I lived in Pallas before Vesta up and moved in ta tha forest. Now ya want to tell me there are two? Get out a here, ya filthy liar."

"I am not lying!!"

"Ya either lied about killing tha first dragon or there is no second one. I haven' decided which, but either way I am done with ya," he said with finality.

"But sir! You may be deliberately ending your life!" Aten said.

There was no answer.

"You cannot remain!" Aten tried again.

Again, no response.

Aten grit his teeth and marched away with frustration, dragging the cart behind him to find guildmates who could break the door down. He wheezed as he brought the weapons with him, but for every strain, he reminded himself how important it would be to have the sword at his side. Unless he met with the dragon, of course.

"Aten," Ren had caught up with him, a sack held over his shoulder, "I thought Boros instructed you to only take the essentials for Waron."

"Waron is acting rashly and not taking anything but these weapons and a few others," Aten said harshly.

"That does sound like Waron," Ren nodded.

"And his neighbor is even worse, insinuating that the whole evacuation is a ruse! He refuses to leave his home! Will you come to help me force him out?" Aten asked.

"That does sound like Unis. It would be a useless endeavor to attempt to bring him with us," Ren replied.

"What? You and I could easily overpower him and make him see reason," Aten countered.

"Yes, physically. But then what? Will we watch him at all hours to ensure he does not flee and return to the village? Or will we tie him up and gag him to stifle his unceasing complaints on how we handled the evacuation?" Ren looked at Aten expectantly and Aten realized they were not rhetorical questions.

"We cannot leave him to die!"

"We are not leaving him to die! He has done that himself by refusing to listen to our warning. His life is left to God now. While I hope he lives, we share no blame if he ends up dead."

Aten took this in and shuddered. He remembered the thrill Vesta would get slaughtering her enemies in battle. He wondered if she had gotten it from her father.

"Allow me to help you with the cart. You are still weak," Ren offered, holding out the light bag over his shoulder to exchange.

"No, this is the payment I promised Waron for my new sword. I wish to carry it through," Aten said, pulling the cart forward despite his muscles protesting in pain.

"Very well," Ren said, walking slowly to keep pace.

They were near the back of a long line of about a hundred villagers leaving their homes carrying what they could on their back. Children protested leaving so soon with such few toys but begrudgingly walked alongside their families. In the front of the crowd, Aten could make out Boros and other knights waving at the villagers to move in an orderly fashion up the hill. From behind them, Aten heard another tree crashing under the weight it could no longer hold in its weakened state. He looked over his shoulder.

He could not help but think the dragon was right behind him. He had no way of knowing how far along it was to finding him.

04

Aten heaved loudly as he dragged the weapons to the highest point of the hill. Ren looked to him with a worried smile. They were approaching Boros and the other knights now, about to make a turn to the evacuation point.

"Are you certain you are up for that?" Ren asked, pointing to the cart with his head.

"Ye—" was all Aten could get out in a breath of air. He groaned as he pulled it to the top, then fell backward, breathing deeply.

"Whoa there, Aten," Boros said, walking over with an arm outstretched, "why don't you let me handle it from here?"

"No," Aten gasped, swallowing hard and shaking his head vigorously. He patted the sword in his sheath and then gesticulated to the weapon cart, trying to communicate the deal he made with Waron.

"Why just the weapons?" Boros asked, first to Aten, then turning to Ren.

"They are Waron's," Ren replied.

"I could have surmised that, but why does Aten not have any supplies of his own?" Boros pointed out. "We can hunt for food, yes, but you cannot hunt for clean clothing or bedding."

"I will be fine," Aten insisted, his breathing more controlled.

"Maybe for now, but you have yet to explain yourself to the guild. We must know what happened and whether you failed to uphold your oath," Boros said.

Aten nodded, still catching his breath. He looked up and noticed he had the perfect view of Pallas. He could see the blazing forest in its transition from fire to embers and ashes now. His eyes spotted the Knight's Guild in the center of town, the farms on the outskirts, and the homes on the small piece of land where families of the past felt fit to settle down. The skies danced with a reverse rain, soot being sucked into the clouds. Aten could not help but look on to the destruction with a faint fascination.

"Would you like me to explain now or on the way to the evacuation point?" he asked, struggling to stand up.

"We are already at the evacuation point, Aten," Ren said, raising an arm to the villagers settling in and setting up tents only a few hundred paces away from where they stood.

"We are... no, this cannot be..." Aten said, looking at them with horror.

"Surprised by how quick we got here?" Boros laughed. "Yes, this is the perfect point to watch an enemy pass through our town while giving us the benefit of the higher ground and the proximity to launch a counterattack. It is fortunate that we live so close to the hill, though our ancestors may have settled here for the reason that the hill was close by."

"This is not enough!" Aten said, panicked.

"What do you mean?" Ren asked.

"We have not fled!" Aten exclaimed. "This distance is nothing to a dragon! It can fly up here and slaughter us in the time it would take for us to draw swords! I thought our evacuation was far beyond the horizons visible to Pallas! No, we must flee!"

Aten looked at the villagers in a daze. So many lives in danger. He began staggering toward them frantically, leaving the cart behind.

"Calm down, Aten," Boros said, pulling on his arm and stopping him. "Do not put the people of Pallas in a state of panic without first explaining yourself."

Aten pulled away from Boros, but his shoulder stung in pain and he remained in his grip. He relaxed his arm and sighed, frustrated.

"I believe there is a dragon coming to Pallas to find me," Aten explained quickly. His breathing was still labored and he could not tell whether it was from exhaustion or fear for the people.

"You swore an oath not to return to Pallas unless a dragon was no longer a burden on this town," Boros said stoically. Aten shivered.

"I killed a dragon. The one residing in the cave, Vesta," Aten explained, panicked.

"There are *more* dragons?" Ren asked skeptically.

"I believe there to be another, yes," Aten said.

"But you killed the first one? The one that was threatening us from the cave?" Boros clarified. Aten frowned. He did not know that he would classify Vesta as threatening the town from her cave, but he felt that this was not the time for technicals.

"Yes, I slew the first dragon. It is her father who must have discovered her body and now comes after me."

"*Must have* discovered her body? Did you not witness this yourself?" Boros asked.

"I—No, I suppose not. I only know that Vesta referred to her father in passing on occasion." Aten remembered having dinner with her, then the tears falling as she lay dying in her lair. He shook the thought out of his head. This was no time to rethink decisions that had been made. He had to deal with the consequences first.

"Knights!" Boros said with command. The knights of the guild looked to him for orders, "Aten fulfilled his oath. He returned when there was no dragon threatening this town. It was only after he returned that a new dragon became a new threat to the town. We are not to carry out any punishment on that oath."

"But Boros, he had not entered Pallas when he began to warn us of the dragon!" a knight nearby protested. "We were still on the outskirts!"

Aten squirmed uncomfortably in place.

"Parner, when we return to our homes, we may discuss the lines that define being within and outside of our town. For now, Aten lives," Boros said with finality. Most knights nodded, appreciating not having to take a life of one of their own, though Parner grumbled to himself.

"Now Aten," Boros said, turning to the young knight, "you believe we should flee from this location?"

"Yes!" Aten said emphatically, "If this new dragon spots us, he can be here before we have time to plan a defense."

"Why can we not defeat it instead? Did you not defeat the first one?" Parner asked accusingly. Aten's vision flashed with his dagger shattering against Vesta's chest.

"Because this dragon's daughter killed all but four of the Royal Guard of the North," Aten rebuked him, "And I was successful because I had time for Vesta to fall—to trust me."

"The Royal Guard of the North..." Ren said with disbelief.

"I heard every Royal Guard of the North can defeat an army of men," Parner said stunned.

"But an army of them could not defeat a dragon," Aten said.

The knights looked in awe. They wondered what kind of events Aten had witnessed to speak so plainly about things they only knew as stories. It was like speaking to a legend.

"Then what is it that we are to do?" Boros asked.

"We—"

Aten whipped around at the sound of the blood-curdling scream of an old man coming from town. The four knights stepped toward the edge of the hill to look down on Pallas. The scream continued, growing more desperate with each moment. Aten's heart went tight as he realized it was Anderson's voice. He stayed true to his word and never left the village.

"It is Aten! The knight Aten is the one you seek! He killed Vesta! Leave me be, demon!" Anderson shouted, his voice quivering through his hysterics.

"We—We have to save him," Parner said quietly, frozen in place.

"We have to run," Aten said, turning around and hobbling over to the village people. "We have to run!" he screamed at them.

The townspeople were looking down on their village, statues in the face of the agonizing cries from their village leader. They did not hear Aten calling to them.

"Tell them to flee!" Aten said, looking back to his guild brothers.

"Right," Boros said, snapping into action. "People of Pallas, we must—"

"Aten!" a voice boomed from the village below. The same voice that had come from the cave earlier. "Aten is the one I seek!"

Aten stared numbly at the town now as Anderson's house flew in every direction in a fiery explosion. In the middle of the inferno, a silhouette of a tall man with wings stood, holding the burning corpse of Anderson.

"I know your name, you murderous knight! I will find you, Aten!" the dragon swore.

05

"By God, what is that thing?" Ren whispered, terrified.

"That is the dragon," Aten declared, staring at the dragon toss Anderson's body aside and walk to the next house in search of him, igniting it in blinding tendrils of fire.

"The man?" Parner said. Aten realized that his guild brothers had never witnessed Vesta and were unfamiliar with dragon-kind.

"That is right. He will look like nothing more than a man with wings. But his skin will shatter a sword, and he is faster than the fastest horse, able to fly from place to place in an instant."

"Then why did it take him so long to make it to Pallas?" Parner asked.

"I do not know. Perhaps he went somewhere else first in search of me," Aten answered as a building below exploded.

"Where?" Parner said.

"*I do not know!*" Aten said impatiently. "We have to flee from here. Now. We cannot defeat it and it will find us soon if we remain up here awaiting his arrival."

Parner swallowed, then nodded. Ren trembled and held his sword tightly, his knuckles whitening and Boros nodded his head and began to walk to the people, then stopped mid step. He stared at the masses ahead of him, then back to Pallas. Another building exploded. The dragon flew into the Knight's Guild.

"Come fight me, Aten! I wish to treat you as you did Vesta!" the dragon called from the building, a deep, enraged roar. Aten swallowed hard.

"We cannot flee," Boros said quietly, his eyes out of focus in thought.

"What!?" Aten said.

"The people of Pallas do not have time to make it out with their lives. If he would take our lives as viciously as he does our village—"

As if to accent his point, the Knight's Guild disintegrated into thousands of ashen splinters.

"Aten!" the dragon blew fire skyward in frustration.

Aten breathed in sharply at the sight of the Knight's Guild as it flew apart. He had nightmares of a dragon destroying his home before. He never considered the dragon would not be Vesta. And he never thought reality would mirror his dream so vividly.

The dragon flew into the next residence. It was the building that Aten had tried to get the man to leave—Unis. The stubborn man began to scream as loud as Elder Anderson did.

"We will be torn apart in the same minute that Aten's life is taken. We cannot flee," Boros said.

"We cannot fight it!" Aten insisted.

"Have you gone mad?" Parner yelled at Boros.

Ren stared at Boros in disbelief, perhaps wondering whether he had lost his sanity after witnessing the raw power of the dragon.

"You would leave the village here to fight rather than give them the chance, however small, to escape?" Ren asked in a small voice.

"No. We, the Knights of Pallas, cannot flee. We must stay and act as a buffer for the villagers to escape. Aten, you will run in a different direction than we send the villagers. We will talk to the dragon long enough to announce that you have fled to the east, while they will travel north," Boros said, looking upon his hometown with dread.

"I can stay and stall him," Aten protested.

"Your ability to fight is not at contention here, it is the fact that we know the dragon searches for you. We will send it in your direction, away from the villagers. Hopefully, the loss of your life will mean an end to its rampage," Boros said, blinking and turning away from the village.

"You—All of the knights will die," Aten said gravely.

"You have such little faith in us? We may be more powerful than Royal Guards of the North! We may yet succeed. Either way, we will live as heroes or die as martyrs," Boros claimed proudly. He ran forward to give commands to the villagers who were still watching in shock as their homes were torn asunder.

"If what Aten says is true… This is suicide," Parner said heavily.

"But we would die so that the village may live. And that is quite the legacy," Ren said lifelessly, tearing his gaze away from the flames to look at his fellow knights. His body trembled aggressively.

"Aten does not have the strength to flee this place at a reasonable pace," Parner said, pointing to Aten's injured leg while his eyes remained on the village.

"Yes, someone would have to carry him," Ren agreed.

"And whoever would be the ones to carry him would likely survive a little longer than the rest of the knights who would stay here to fight the dragon," Parner suggested.

"I suppose so," Ren agreed, a drop of energy entering his voice.

Aten watched them closely as he came to understand what they were discussing. They did not want to remain and fight.

"We can all flee," Aten said carefully. "We can all escape from here so long as we leave before the dragon thinks to come up the hill."

"Aten!!" the dragon roared, tearing through more houses while billowing smoke and fire across the grounds.

"You said it yourself, Aten," Parner said with a deadpan voice. "The dragon could be here the moment it decides to be up here. You should leave now. Ren and I could help you make your escape."

"I am not escaping," Aten protested, "I am the next target as soon as the dragon is done here!"

"Yes, and whoever is here will be done," Parner said.

Boros came back to the three knights with a hand outstretched to grasp Aten's forearm.

"Aten, you were a wonderful brother. I am honored to fight for a Dragonslayer in what may be my last hour. Now leave! The villagers are already making their way north. Go east now, and be sure to leave signs of your exit."

"Boros, Ren and I were thinking that we should be alongside Aten to speed up his escape on account of his unusable leg!" Parner blurted out. Ren did not nod, nor did he refute the claim. He shook with fear.

"I can use my leg!" Aten said scowling at Parner.

"No, he is right Aten. It would be good that you make as good a distance as you can in what is such an uncertain span of time. In fact..."

Boros turned Waron's cart of weapons over, emptying it. He gestured for Aten to get inside.

"Boros, I made an agreement with Waron that—"

"Aten we do not have time for this!" Parner insisted, getting behind and hoisting him inside the cart.

"Unfortunately, Parner is right. You must go now," Boros said compassionately, pushing the cart off. "If the dragon does not notice us, we will return to the people of Pallas in the north. We directed them to the city of Kit. Should you find yourself unfollowed, you may meet with us there."

"Boros wait!" Aten said, pulling him in close and whispering. "Ren and Parner only wish to help me so that they may flee the coming battle. They are... They are not acting as Knights of the Guild should."

"Given the circumstances, I do not blame them," Boros whispered back, winking and patting Aten on his good shoulder.

"Godspeed Boros!" Parner said, pulling the cart with Aten away as fast as he could.

"Godspeed my brothers! May we meet again!" Boros said, waving farewell.

Aten watched Boros and the other knights he grew up with drift further from view as Ren and Parner exchanged pulling the cart at the fastest speed they could muster. Aten felt a wave of relief as the last villager left his eyeline, each of them at least beginning the journey in safety. The plan may work after all.

The hill turned from an overlook to a horizon as he was pulled a great distance; the only sign of Pallas were the small shapes of knights on the hill waiting their adversary and the giant funnel of smoke overtaking the sky, blocking out the setting sun. Just as Aten started believing the dragon might have left without causing harm to anyone who left the village, he saw a blast of fire at the center of the knights.

The dragon had arrived at the top of the hill.

N. T. Lazer

06

Aten could not make out the figures on the horizon fighting with the dragon due to both distance he had taken in the cart and the overwhelming smoke in the air. He squinted, trying hard to get a glimpse of the knights fighting the dragon off, but the most he could make out was the passing silhouette at the edge of the smoke, disappearing as quickly as it would appear. The cart shook violently as it was dragged over rocks on the ground; he winced, as his injured leg flared up in pain.

"Can we move slower?" Aten asked.

Parner looked at him disdainfully with the small bag of supplies they had over his shoulder. Ren only frowned, focusing on the task of pulling Aten in the cart.

"We are trying to make as much distance between the villagers we are sworn to protect and you wish for us to slow down?" Parner asked, wiping sweat from his brow.

"Is the distance for the sake of the villagers or for the sake of prolonging our lives?" Aten asked accusationally.

"Ah! You have discovered my secret Aten! I do not want to die by being torn in twain at the hands of a ruthless monster. Go ahead and mock, I give you my full permission," Parner said with contempt.

Aten sat with his arms crossed, trying to think of something to say to better make his point, but Parner left him with little to work with. It furthered his feeling of a lack of autonomy. Dragons. They left little control in the hands of man. He was not even sure that a strike to the heart would kill this one. He was still unclear whether the message was literal or metaphorical when discussing the "vulnerable" heart strike needed to defeat a dragon. He wished there was another way to defeat dragons. But he did not have any information on how to accomplish such a feat. He only knew of one man that did.

"We should visit Pirulo, the bard of old," Aten announced to his companions.

"Aten, I do not know if you have already gone mad, but we are not in a position to be able to drop by anywhere for visits, in case you were unaware," Parner said, exasperated.

"But we may be able to discover a way to defeat the dragon if we see the bard. He is a man of great wisdom. We should go in search of him in the Deserted Desert, in case we are able to find him before the dragon finds us," Aten said.

"We will not be able to escape it," Ren said suddenly, breathing heavily as he pulled. "We are leaving tracks with this cart."

Aten looked at the land they had traversed and now noticed the fine grooves in the ground, a ledger tracking every rotation of the wheels.

"Then we can leave the cart behind to be the bait for the dragon, and start to travel on foot," Aten said.

"No, if the dragon is as fast as you say, it will simply fly upward and locate us in seconds after seeing where the cart has been abandoned," Ren was quick to say.

"Well," Parner sighed, tapping Ren on the shoulder to trade places with him pulling the cart, "I did not wish to die today."

"We may escape it yet," Ren said, taking the bag of supplies and pulling out bread to hand to Aten.

"How?" Aten asked, holding the bread confused as Parner grunted as he began to pull the cart.

"We are moving uphill. There will eventually be a point where uphill turns to downhill. We may be able to push the cart down, leaving the grooves to lead the dragon beyond where we are hidden," Ren explained.

"A nice dream, but the cart leaves marks in the earth because of Aten's weight. Much as I would love it, I am doubtful that Aten would sit idle in a cart rolling downhill," Parner said, turning his neck to see

Aten's response. Aten shook his head. Parner shrugged.

"We could fill it with dirt or clay from the earth," Aten suggested.

"No," Ren said, "that would inform the dragon of where we stopped to gather dirt and he would simply look from that point. We must be more subtle. We will leave the bag of supplies in your stead, Aten."

"What?" Parner exclaimed.

"Get out of the cart, Aten," Ren ordered. Aten looked between the two knights, then back at the wall of smoke where the dragon remained.

"Ren, how are we going to eat if—"

"Parner, we do not have time to discuss details. The beast could be upon us at any moment and this plan works better if we act now," Ren said, looking at Aten pointedly. Aten slowly pulled himself out of the cart.

"Take off your boots and head to that tree, hiding out of sight from this path," Ren said, pointing to a small smatter of plantlife far off the path.

"But what will—"

"Parner and I will run up the hill as fast as we can and send the cart down from wherever the highest point is, away from the tree. If we are fortunate enough to do all of that before the dragon arrives, we will join you. Try not to eat all the bread at once, it is all the food we will have," Ren said, pushing Parner to begin pulling the cart again.

"Oh, I hate this plan," Parner said reluctantly, sprinting further up the path with Ren close behind.

"Wait, but…" Aten began, but they ignored him. So much of his journey had been alone. He did not want to lose more of his friends to dragons. He breathed and began limping to the foliage, flipping his head worriedly between the smokescreen where the dragon was fighting the knights and his comrades running up the path. His leg and shoulder burned with every infinitesimal movement of his body.

Finally, he reached the tree and collapsed behind it, caked in sweat. He breathed deeply and took a small, yet ravenous bite from the bread. He looked back to the direction of Pallas and saw nothing but smoke. With a tightness in his stomach, he looked up, finally considering that the dragon may be searching from far above the land. Still nothing. He sighed and looked to Ren and Parner. They had stopped running and were looking down at what must have been the peak of his hill. They made it in time.

Aten wondered why this dragon had yet to emerge from the smoke. Was it possible that Boros and the other knights were able to hold off the dragon? Did they strike its heart by accident and defeat it? The seed of hope grew ever-so-slightly in Aten's heart. Parner and Ren pushed the cart down and began running perpendicular to its direction, toward Aten.

Aten looked back to Pallas and was blinded immediately. Adjusting his view, he saw a searing white flame coming from just within the smoke, bright enough to make him have to cover the sight with one hand. Soon, it emerged from the smoke behind a man flying not far from the ground. The hope Aten felt died all at once.

The dragon.

It approached them slower than Aten would have expected, but at a voracious speed nonetheless. He realized that the dragon was flying slowly in order to properly cover the ground in flames. It was razing the land while in pursuit.

Turning his head back to Parner and Ren he saw them looking at the dragon, stunned. They were still fully in view. They were right in the path of the column of flames approaching.

07

"Run!" Aten screamed.

Parner and Ren were stuck in awe, staring numbly at the great wall of flame coming at them.

"What are you doing? Run!" Aten screamed louder. He looked around him for a rock to throw. There was nothing other than leaves and dried roots. He saw his boots on the ground next to him. He shook the idea away as soon as it came. He would need those. Then, he looked to the bread in his hands. His stomach growled.

Aten frowned his hunger away and crushed the bread, wadding it up into a tight ball and throwing it as hard as he could at his brethren. It bounced off Parner's head. Parner blinked, dumbfounded, then slapped the back of Ren's head and continued his run to where Aten lay hidden. Ren was quick to follow.

Aten looked back at the dragon, sweating as it drew closer. It was impossible to tell where it was looking. If it saw them running, it would incinerate them in an instant. He remembered how fast the Romsons were burned alive by Vesta. So fast, they did not have the time to react to the pain before death overcame them. He did not even remember if their bodies remained.

"Faster!" Aten screamed at his friends frantically.

"Yes, I know!" Parner screamed back, tripping over his armor.

Ren was looking to the ground as he ran, focusing only on escaping.

Aten looked once more at the dragon, then looked away shielding his eyes. It was far too bright to look at directly now that it had closed three fourths of the distance. He could feel the heat from the white flames being spewed from the monster. Aten knew that if the dragon saw his comrades ahead of it, he would be killed along with them, given how large the column of flame was. But he knew the plan was to die here, alongside his brothers for the safety of his village. He only wished Boros was right and that the dragon would be satisfied with his death.

Parner and Ren collapsed behind him, breathing hard and looking over his shoulder.

"Do not look directly at it, for it is blinding," Aten warned.

"I only care to know if the dragon saw us!" Parner said urgently.

Aten chanced a glance. The dragon would either be upon them or passing them in seconds. If it passed him without noticing, then Boros and the other knights' sacrifice would be in vain. He stood up with the help of the plant he hid behind.

"What are you doing?" Parner hissed, his brow drenched in sweat as the heat continued to become more extreme.

"I am going out there," Aten declared, taking a step toward outside of the small hidden area.

"Are you mad?" Parner screamed.

"Parner it is for the—"

Aten gasped as he fell to the ground, tackled by Ren.

"Ren what are you—"

"You wish to sacrifice yourself so that the dragon might stop its rampage?" Ren asked, drops of sweat falling from his head.

"Yes! I may be able to save everyone if—"

"If the dragon did not see us hide in this light cover, what makes you believe it would notice if it incinerated you right now? Who knows where the dragon is looking? If the dragon saw us, it will confront us and you may have the martyrdom you seek. If it did not, then it will likely not see you as it kills you," Ren said.

Aten did not even have the time to react to that information before he had to screw his eyes shut as the blinding flames passed by the three of them, leaving a merciless heat behind. They breathed laboriously, Ren and Parner from their run and Aten from the heat that encompassed them all.

"Ren, why did you—"

"The tree is on fire!" Parner yelled pointing.

Aten looked up to see embers on a branch crawling toward him, approaching as fast as they could muster.

"Ren!" Aten yelled.

Ren was still pinning him down. Ren pulled him up and threw him at Parner's feet who in turn picked Aten up to his feet immediately. The three of them tripped and stumbled away from the fire as it dragged itself toward them, jumping from branch to tree to bush.

"Why are they all catching flame so quickly?" Aten panted.

"The dragon dehydrated everything with its blast," Ren answered.

Aten licked his lips and felt cracks all over them. His tongue had no moisture to add to them. He stumbled back in panic as the flames continued to make their way, gaining on the trio. Aten was dead weight. He needed to be left behind.

"Go ahead and run," Aten said bravely.

Parner looked at him, wide eyed.

"Very well, but this may hurt with your shoulder injured," Ren said.

"What—"

Ren folded his arms under Aten's and ran, pulling him along as if hoisting a sack. Aten gritted his teeth as the pain overwhelmed him. He could hear Parner running alongside them until he decided to pick up Aten's legs, easing the strain on Ren. Aten watched the fire fall behind as the two carried him off. He tried to sigh in relief but only coughed in pain.

"Put me down, put me down, we have placed enough distance," Aten pleaded.

"Enough distance that we can catch you before you try to walk into these flames?" Parner teased.

"Parner," Ren warned as he stood Aten up and the three began walking and limping away from the way the dragon had gone.

The three looked at one another, then out at the dragon that was making its way downhill, the stream of fire constant.

"My God, it can just spit fire like a waterfall," Parner observed. "And the heat of it! Did you see how the land he burned turned black even before the flame reached it. I dare say if we were only a few inches closer we would be welded to our armors."

Aten gave the land a good look. A dark, lifeless scar was scratched in black on the ground leaving nothing but the memory of destruction in its wake. He looked as far as he could back in the direction of Pallas and saw the abrasion the whole way to the horizon. Even the tree they had just taken shelter behind had wilted into a black twig.

"I am sorry that I brought this beast upon us," Aten said, sighing.

"Aten, let this be the end of your feeling of guilt, otherwise you may have us killed," Ren chastised. Parner looked at him interested.

"What do you mean? I brought this dragon here by killing Vesta! And we never knew Vesta to leave her forest!" Aten protested.

"Yes, but we knew Vesta to kill those who entered her forest. Had you not vanquished Vesta, one who came after you eventually would. And if you continue to wallow in your guilt and insecurities, you will surely needlessly risk your life once again, just as you did when the dragon was passing and just as you did when the flames were hot on our heels. Yes, the original plan was that we may all be sacrificed, but that plan is no longer viable. Do not use it as an excuse to kill yourself. Leave this feeling of guilt behind," Ren repeated.

"But—"

"Aten do not speak until you are once again of sound mind of a knight," Ren ordered.

Aten stared at him dumbfounded. Ren had never spoken to him in this way, but he had also never been in a dire situation alongside him. He watched his feet as he tried to follow the direction of thought. Leave his guilt behind. This dragon was not his fault. Vesta had killed Roth, all of the fighters alongside Tholen, and even the merchant and his young daughter. Aten killed a monster. But he brought one much worse.

Parner spoke up,

"What are we supposed to do while A—"

"Parner, it would do us all well to be silent for a moment. Let Aten reflect in peace and then we can make a plan," Ren said curtly, holding up a hand to silence him.

Parner opened his mouth as if to reply then closed it and grumbled something to himself.

Aten continued down his mental path. This monster was brought on by his actions. But had he not taken those actions, there was no telling how many of Aten's friends and brethren Vesta would have killed as Pallas's neighbor. This new dragon may have come eventually. It was clearly much more bold and aggressive than Vesta ever was, so it took little imagination to believe it may have done this for any number of reasons.

It was not his fault.

He was one of many reasons that the dragon may have come out to attack the world.

It was not his fault.

He breathed out, not realizing he had been holding his breath.

"Better?" Ren asked.

"Yes, thank you, Ren," Aten said gratefully.

"Now that Aten is no longer suicidal," Parner began.

"I was never sui—"

"—what are we going to do?"

"We go to see Pirulo," Aten said.

"What, the bard of old?" Parner asked, disappointed.

"That is right, he may have the information we need to defeat this new dragon. He instructed me on how to kill Vesta," Aten said. He was satisfied to realize this was the first time he mentioned killing her without a rock forming in his stomach.

"But you said he is in the Deserted Desert!" Parner whined.

"I know how to find him," Aten assured him.

"Find him! Ha! The Deserted Desert is at least a half day's trek from here, I am more worried that starvation will find us before we find him! Need I remind you that the only supplies we have remaining are a loaf of bread and the weapons in our sheathes?" Parner asked.

"Oh... well, actually I threw the loaf of bread at you when I—"

Parner groaned loudly, rubbing his temples.

"Fine. Supplies first, then we find Pirulo," Aten conceded.

08

Aten lagged behind Parner and Ren who dutifully watched the horizon as they continued through the plantlife. Ren cut any trees or bushes that looked like it would give Aten trouble and Parner would continue to remind the trio that he was hungry and wanted to eat. Aten noticed with some gratitude that he did not feel as inclined to limp as he did before. He tenderly touched his shoulder and felt much less pain than he normally did. He was healing.

"How long until we reach the town of Kit?" Aten asked.

"Kit!" Parner laughed. "Where do you think we are?"

Aten frowned.

"East of Pallas," he answered, somewhat offended.

"That is right. And where is Kit?"

"I know it lies north of Pallas, Parner, do not patronize me. Are we not traveling north?" Aten retorted.

"We are, yes, but Kit would be more accurately described as northwest of Pallas. A few days' journey. With the lack of supplies and..." he gestured to Aten's injured leg, "we will not make it by the time we will be in need of a meal. There should be smaller villages in the immediate area. And hopefully an animal will cross our paths that I can eat. I am famished."

"You are? I had not realized after the first dozen times you said it," Aten grumbled sarcastically.

"Apologies, Aten, but who was it that needed to be carted out of a village, draining me of my strength and bringing on this great hunger of mine?" Parner asked brazenly.

"Oh, him?" Aten asked impudently, "I believe it was *the Dragonslayer*. A hero who risked his life to save the village!"

"Hero?" Parner spat. "What have you done except bring us from one misfortune to ano—"

Parner stopped when he saw Ren had turned around to stare at the two of them. Aten grabbed an arm awkwardly and looked to the floor. Parner swallowed whatever else he planned to say.

"We are brothers. Act like it," Ren said simply.

Aten and Parner looked to one another, neither offering an apology. Ren sighed and continued,

"Parner, Aten slayed a dragon not more than a moon ago and already you speak to him without respect. You are fortunate he does not ask you to refer to him as Dragonslayer, being that he has earned the title."

Aten nodded to Parner who shrugged noncommittally.

"And Aten," Ren spoke, "be easy on Parner. He has only today witnessed the horrors of a dragon. He and I will need time to adjust to the new world."

Aten sighed and nodded to Ren.

"Apologies, Parner, I did not mean to aggravate you," Aten said, holding out a hand.

"I am sorry as well Aten. I cannot imagine what goes through the mind of someone who killed a dragon and witnessed its ferocity firsthand," Parner returned the handshake.

Ren nodded at them and continued walking forward.

"I too, cannot imagine that which you have experienced, Aten. It may do us well if you were to describe your experience to us so that we may be better informed on the new dragon threat," Ren suggested.

Aten swallowed. He was not sure he was ready to talk about how he killed Vesta after gaining her trust. He was also uncomfortable sharing the details of the final battle between Tholen, himself, and the Royal Guard of the North. He had done nothing but deliver the final blow, after dozens of men were killed in battle with Vesta. He could have stopped it sooner. And he could have saved Roth's life.

Aten stopped and winced when Parner suddenly pulled him by the shoulder.

"Parner, that is my injured should—"

"Shh!" Parner held a hand up to Aten then pointed silently to a rabbit eating grass at the base of a tree no more than five paces away, its eyes unfocused.

"Has it seen us?" Ren whispered.

Parner held up his hand to silence him as well, then shrugged. The three knights watched the rabbit chewing quickly and envied its filling stomach. Parner knelt down and picked up a rock, weighing it in his hands, then slowly brought it back, preparing to throw it. The two watched carefully as Parner concentrated and closed one eye taking careful aim. He breathed in slowly and a low grumble suddenly broke his focus.

His own stomach.

The rabbit's head whipped in their direction and registered them as predators, dashing away.

"Wonderful!" Parner yelled sarcastically, throwing the rock at the rabbit. It bounced off the earth next to it, a near miss.

"No!" Aten yelled, drawing his sword and whipping it at the animal. A part of the blade connected with it, and the rabbit tumbled to one side, yelping in surprise. It got up and yelped again. It began hobbling away, only having use of three of its paws.

Ren and Parner looked at Aten, impressed, as Aten stared at the rabbit equally surprised.

"Bless you Aten. Bless you and your recklessness," Parner praised, running ahead and pulling his own sword to finish off the creature. He held it up for his friends to see, beaming.

"Lunch!" he said excitedly.

"More like dinner," Ren said, gesturing to the length of the trees' shadows.

Parner nodded and picked up Aten's sword, hurrying back to the duo.

"Shall we stop here for the night, then?" Parner asked excitedly.

"I thought we were searching for a place to stay?" Aten asked.

"Not when we have food!" Parner said, his stomach agreeing.

"Parner, you are letting your hunger cloud your judgement," Ren admonished. "Though, I agree. We can stop in the next clearing we find and give Aten some much needed rest for his injuries."

"And eat," Parner nodded, taking the lead to hack away everything standing between him and dinner.

"We still do not have anything to drink." Aten poked at his cracked lips.

"Yes. But a meal without water is better than none. And the capture of this rabbit is good news! It means that it must have a water source nearby. We can go in search of it in daylight. For now, you tell us everything you know about dragons," Ren answered.

Aten was grateful to finally have some rest, but was worried about having to speak. He did not want them to think him such a weak knight that he could not fend for himself at all in the course of the battle. He wished he had acted differently. And somewhere in the back of his mind, he still questioned whether killing Vesta was the right thing to do after all. He would always need to remind himself that she killed two innocents for no reason—the merchant and his young daughter, Didra.

"A clearing. Just up ahead," Parner called, cutting an errant branch and picking it up. "I will start the fire!"

Aten and Ren entered the small clearing and were satisfied to find it somewhat concealing on all ends. Ren quickly went to assist Parner in gathering wood and told Aten to sit down and rest. Aten did so without hesitation, his injuries flaring with the day's experience behind them.

Shadows melded together into a coat of darkness as the sun departed from the sky. Aten watched as Parner swore at the sticks in hand, struggling to get them lit.

"Need assistance?" Ren asked.

"No, I—" he focused on the task, his stomach completing the sentence.

"I can start the fire," Ren offered.

"*I* can start a fire!" Parner spat, staring angrily at the twigs. "If only I could…"

"Breathe fire?" Aten teased.

"What, like a dragon? And incinerate our food? No, definitely not," he shook his head, rubbing the sticks more vigorously.

Aten thought back to the meal he and Vesta shared. It left him with a bittersweet feeling.

"Dragons can adjust the heat of their flame. Just as one can melt the leaves off a tree, it can cook a cut of meat to perfection," Aten said.

Parner laughed.

"It is not a joke, Parner," Aten said.

"And how would you know of their ability to cook? Did you dine with one?" Parner said with a wide smile.

Aten looked to the floor.

"Aten, did you dine with one?" he repeated, this time serious.

"I did."

Parner stopped trying to start the fire and looked up to Ren. Ren blinked, dumbfounded at the information.

"You are serious?" Ren inquired cautiously.

Aten nodded.

"By God!" Parner blurted. "Ren, you start the fire. I will start cooking so that Aten may be comfortable enough to regale us of his tale."

"Parner, I am not sure I—"

"Aten, I will not feed you until you go through the story of how you had dinner with a dragon in which you were not the meal," Parner said, waving the dead rabbit enticingly.

Aten said nothing and Parner nodded to himself, satisfied, before skinning the rabbit. Within a minute, Ren was able to start a fire, and given another minute, had it large enough to warm the three of them. He stoked it while Parner stabbed pieces of meat into twig skewers and held them over the flame. They both looked up to Aten expectantly. Aten squirmed in place.

"Anytime now Aten," Parner said.

Aten's face grew pale.

"What ails you, Aten? You need not be embarrassed of anything you have to share with us. We are brothers," Ren implored.

Aten saw the hunger for knowledge in his eyes, but behind that was genuine compassion. He looked to Parner who nodded encouragingly.

"Very well," Aten conceded.

Through the course of the meal, Aten was able to relay the entirety of his experience with Vesta. Many times, Parner opened his mouth as if to ask a question or make a comment, but he was too curious to stop Aten for any point of information. Aten went through the whole tale, leaving nothing out, as much as it mortified him to do so. From their first encounter, to the melodic advice of Pirulo the bard. The invincibility of dragons and the weapons he lost along the way. Of Tholen and his crew and how they were killed mercilessly. How Pallas treated Aten like an enemy and Vesta took him as an ally. The army slain at the mouth of her lair. The death of their guild brother Roth. And the death of Vesta with the profession of love.

Aten's face was flush by the end of it, embarassed by how he seemed powerless to the end, and how only her affection for him let her guard down enough for him to attack. But after completing the story with the entrance of her father, he felt cathartic. He had never had the chance to fully explain himself before, and having people to share it with made him more comfortable with his experience.

"By God, you are an honest Dragonslayer, Aten," Parner said with wonder, sitting up from his reclined position against a stone.

Ren nodded in proud agreement, closing his mouth which he realized had been hanging open.

"I understand your hesitations now. The dragon seemed... almost understandable. Except the killing. So much death surrounded it. The poor merchant and his daughter," Ren said softly.

The three watched the flames for a few seconds in thought.

"There are some things I do not quite understand," Ren said, scratching his chin.

"Yes, what did the dragon see in you?" Parner teased.

Aten could not help but laugh.

"Why was it that Vesta fell in the end? Pirulo told you to strike a vulnerable heart. Did he mean to speak literally and strike her with a blade or did he mean to betray her when she trusted you?" Ren continued.

"I know not. If he meant it metaphorically, then why would her father still live? Would he not be brokenhearted at the sight of his daughter?" Aten replied.

"Perhaps he is filled with unbridled rage and seeks nothing but revenge," Parner spoke through bits of rabbit in his mouth.

"Or perhaps dragons grieve differently than we do," Ren suggested.

"Vesta acted much like a young woman normally would. I would not expect them to have a different set of emotions," Aten thought out loud.

"Curse the bards and their cryptic speech!" Parner said, swallowing his last bit of meat and laying back against the stone.

The three of them watched the fire in silence for a few minutes. Watching it made Aten wonder where the dragon was now. If it had stopped burning the land. Whether it still searched for them. How long they had to live.

"You believe Pirulo will have the answer to how to defeat this monster?" Ren asked.

"Not you, too," Parner groaned.

"I do," Aten nodded seriously. "He was able to tell me what I needed to know to defeat Vesta. He may know what to do differently with her father."

"And what if he tells you the same information?" Parner said, throwing his arms open. "You would have us travel all the way South, back in the direction we know the dragon to be, to the Deserted Desert on a *supposition* of assistance. We do not know what may come of it!"

"Exactly, we do not know what wisdom he holds," Aten agreed.

Parner ran his hands through his hair.

"That was not meant to be a point in your favor!" he yelled.

"What would you have us do, Parner? What better idea do you have?"

"My idea is one of practicality. Go to Kit and find our people. Live the rest of our lives. The world is massive, Aten. It is unlikely we will ever cross paths with it again. It will not even know where to search for us!" Parner insisted.

"What if it burns every tow—"

"Save your strength," Ren told the two of them, holding up a hand before they ran further down the path of argument. "Let us get sleep now and we can discuss our next moves at first light."

Parner and Aten nodded reluctantly, though Aten felt his eyes droop as soon as he was no longer speaking. He knew sleep would come easy when covered in this blanket of exhaustion. He laid back and closed his eyes, hearing the other two do the same. He thought of this new dragon. And Vesta. Aten's thoughts were soon replaced with dreams.

He sat with Vesta at a dinner table in a castle. They were both dressed formally, eating meat Aten had brought them. They were eating rabbit that she cooked by her own flame. Rabbit was her favorite.

"Where did you get your dress?" Aten asked.

Vesta gestured behind him.

Turning around, Aten saw her father sitting on the throne, his body engulfed in flames. Aten's eyes went wide and he got up to run, but his injured leg kept him from making any distance.

"I have found you Aten!" the dragon screamed, leaping forward.

Aten awoke to a net falling over him, pinning him to the ground.

09

"Who—What is happening?" Parner asked before being ensnared by another net appearing from nowhere.

"Hey!" Aten cried, regaining his senses and struggling against his bonds, "Ambush!"

Ren rolled on the ground, narrowly avoiding a third net and drawing his sword, only to be hit in the head by a rock. He grabbed his forehead in pain and was unable to deflect the second net that came down and captured him.

"Are you free?" Parner asked, twisting his head to get a view of him.

"They have immobilized me as well," Aten said, trying to get a clear view in the dark night. Only the slight embers of the remaining fire illuminated shadowy figures on the outskirts of their clearing.

"Who immobilized us?" Parner said, annoyed.

"Good work," a voice said, entering the clearing.

Emerging from the shadows as if exiting a lake of black water, a woman holding a bow appeared.

"An archer," Aten said, angrily.

"Great," Parner said, struggling to angle his arm to try and reach the sword he had set next to him while he slept. "A woman."

The sword he reached for was kicked away by the young woman, followed by the three of them being slowly dragged by hidden figures into the shadow.

"What will we do with them, Trise?" another woman's voice asked from somewhere out of view.

"Take care not to harm them unless they give us a struggle. I think these men are suited for trade in Berdun," Trise said, walking alongside them. She had collected their weapons.

"Berdun? If you want us to last that long, you will have to give us water soon. We are quite parched," Parner said, already lounging in his net.

"Parner," Aten said, attempting to silence him.

"What? If we are going to be captives, why not try getting something out of it," Parner said.

"We do not even know who they are," Aten said, looking to Ren.

Ren pressed a hand to his forehead, stopping blood from coming out. He looked somberly to Aten, but said nothing. Aten understood. He did not want to reveal anything unnecessary to them.

Trise watched them intently.

"Where are the rest of your belongings?" she asked.

"You are holding them," Parner said immediately.

"Parner!" Aten said.

"Where is your food? Your finances?" Trise asked, this time speaking directly to Parner.

"In your hands," Parner said.

Aten stopped protesting, seeing he was not getting through to him.

"You expect us to believe that you are traveling with nothing but swords and the clothes on your backs?" Trise asked skeptically.

"Armor on our backs, actually," Parner corrected.

Aten groaned.

"Armor? I thought that was what it was, but it must not be very useful seeing the wounds on your friend here," she said, pointing to Aten's shoulder and calf with his own sword.

"Yes, we are from a small village. Our Knight's Guild is not equipped with the most protective armor, just enough for small scraps and skirmishes," Parner explained.

"What village would that be?" Trise asked.

"Why are you looking to take us to Berdun?" Parner asked, rolling over in his net to get a better look at Trise while being dragged along.

She frowned at him, shaking her head.

"I am asking questions, where are you from, Parner?" she asked, more aggressively this time.

"Yes, and I am tired of giving answers. I am more in the mood to ask questions now. Why Berdun?" Parner said without missing a beat.

"Why are you traveling with so few belongings?" Trise asked, not directing the question to Parner anymore.

"Where are you from?" Parner responded.

"What are your names?" Trise asked Aten and Ren.

"How old are you?" Parner said, throwing her off again.

"Stop talking!" she demanded.

"Best of luck with that," Ren spoke.

Aten stifled a laugh.

Trise looked between the three of them, taken aback.

"Are you all mad? Are you so comfortable in a state of defeat, even when you are knights?" Trise asked.

"This is hardly a defeat—ouch," Parner said, his net running over a pile of rocks.

"Hardly a—What do you think is happening right now?" she asked.

"We watched our village as it was burned to the ground just hours ago. This does not compare," Parner said sullenly.

"Burned to the ground? Did a pack of bandits come your way? Has Torn declared war?" she asked, suddenly serious.

"It was a dragon," Parner said.

The people dragging the net slowed down for a moment, turning around to look at Trise.

"That is… not possible. Vesta has left her lair?" she asked.

"You knew Vesta?" Aten asked.

"*Knew?* I know of her, yes," Trise said.

"This one here killed her," Parner pointed.

"Parner!" Aten screamed in protest.

"You *what?*" Trise yelled.

The nets stopped moving.

"You… you are a Dragonslayer?" one of the girls dragging them asked.

No one responded.

"Ladies, we have done it," Trise declared. "Sell these boys to Berdun and we are set for life."

10

"Slavery?" Aten asked, more than a little disappointed he found himself in slave traders' hands.

"Berdun prides itself on its entertainment, not its labor," Trise answered with a smirk.

"Ah, they are full of jugglers, then? I am a fine juggler, myself," Parner said smugly.

Trise rolled her eyes.

"Entertainment of a different caliber," she clarified with a sly expression.

"Do you enjoy speaking in half-answers?" Parner asked disdainfully, "You want us to continue asking until we reach the terrifying conclusion? You then want us to bemoan the fact that we will be put into a ring to fight others to the death? Let me attempt a gaze of terror."

Parner raised his eyebrows and widened his eyes.

"How did I do?" he asked.

"Quiet," Trise frowned, her face a light shade of red now.

"Fighting in a ring?" Aten asked.

"Try not to think too hard about it. It is still slaves, but your duty is to kill other slaves. Berdun is infamous for it," Parner explained.

"How disgusting," Aten shook his head. "Why would I matter in that case?"

"How humble," Trise said, "the Dragonslayer does not think he would sell well as a fighter."

"You mean, you believe the Dragonslayer is the best of us at fighting?" Parner exclaimed, laughing. "Just yesterday he threw a sword at a rabbit to catch it! Why, I could probably best him unarmed while he fought fully equipped."

"I said be quiet!" Trise yelled at him.

"Are you unaware there is another dragon hunting him down?" Parner asked.

Trise's face was a mix of confusion and frustration, combatting the feeling of wanting Parner's silence and wanting to know more.

"You slay one dragon and you come to me with stories of another? I know Vesta lived alone."

"You were so eager to believe he was able to slay the dragon, but not willing to accept that there is another?" Parner asked, protecting his head from another pile of rocks he was being dragged over.

"That was different, you had no reason to lie then," Trise said.

"Oh, yes, and the circumstances have changed drastically now," Parner agreed.

"I said shut up!" Trise said, raising one of the swords she held, then stopping herself from hitting him.

"Cannot hit the items of sale, can you?" Parner teased.

"Trise, stop speaking with them," the one dragging Parner suggested.

"I know what I am doing," Trise snapped.

Aten looked to Ren, hoping to get a signal or advice on what to do, but Ren was absorbing the conversation stoically, rubbing the bruises that were forming as a result of being dragged through the rough terrain of the forest. He noticed that Ren did not look upset that Parner was speaking to their captors as much as he was.

"The dragon is Vesta's father, actually," Parner continued.

"This becomes more believable with every sentence," Trise said sarcastically.

"Yes, he went on a rampage yesterday. Burned down Pallas and then went on to burn half of this very forest," Parner pointed.

The one dragging Aten paused in thought. She spoke slowly as the pieces fell together in her mind.

"The fire we saw at sunset last night... That was—"

"Gertrude, what would a captive do except speak lies?" Trise said, chastising her.

"Why else was there such flames yesterday? We saw the smoke in the southeast! A cloud of ash," Gertrude said, worried.

"The southeast? You likely mean our village, Pallas," Parner nodded.

"Shut your mouth before I shut it for you," Trise warned him. Parner smiled.

"Trise, how else do you believe the smoke manifested? What kind of people would burn so much when they could just occupy the village for themselves? Pallas is a farming society, if I recall correctly," Gertrude continued.

"Enough! Stop trying to rationalize their lies into your fears. Regardless of the circumstances, it does not change the fact that we are selling them to Berdun!" Trise yelled.

"Even if that dragon has vowed to hunt me down?" Aten asked. He eyed her bow distastefully.

Trise did not respond.

"I may be able to defeat it, you know. But you would have to let me go. Let us all go," Aten said.

The three pulling the knights slowed their speed and turned to look at Trise. She pursed her lips in thought.

"We are selling them in Berdun. That is my final decision. We will rest at home for a few hours, then head out when the sun can better light our way."

The three nodded, followed by continuing to drag them. Parner opened his mouth again, but Trise was quick to place a blade at his lips. He shrugged, smiling.

As they continued their path to captivity, the three pulling the knights were swapped out with another three who were following them in the treeline. Aten could make out a total of ten people in total in this ambush, all of them women of varying age. While Trise was definitely the leader of this group, he was unable to tell whether they were part of a larger village or if they were just a traveling band of slavers. Parner attempted to start conversations a number of times, but was either met with silence or a threat from Trise, none of which were carried out. Aten longed to stop being dragged, as the pain was getting to be unbearable on his shoulder. It had been at least an hour. Without his armor, he suspected he would be nothing but sores and open skin all over. With the armor, however, he was a mass of bruises.

"Can we stop, please? My wounds may be reopening," Aten asked, embarrassed to be asking anything of Trise.

"Yes, a chance to get up, stretch, and relieve ourselves would be a great idea," Parner agreed.

Trise wiped sweat from her brow.

"Tell me your names, and I will give you respite, I suppose," Trise suggested.

Aten looked at her skeptically.

"How can we trust you to—"

"This one is Roth and the other Boros," Parner said immediately.

"Parner!" Ren said angrily.

"Yes, thank you Boros, and I am Parner," Parner completed.

Aten was stunned at his ability to lie so seamlessly.

"Very well, we will be arriving in just a minute. We will free you just up ahead," Trise said, smiling.

"Ah…" Parner sighed, "It seems we would have been freed if only we could have a minute's more patience, *Roth*." He turned to stare disdainfully at Aten.

Aten tried to shrug, but his body did not feel up to the task.

Sure enough, in a few seconds' time, they had sight of a small village. They were pulled forward to a shed and in a matter of minutes, they were bound by the arms and legs tightly with rope and freed from their nets. It took them a slightly longer period of time to tie up Ren, for he was squirming a bit more than Aten or Parner did. Like sacks of wheat, they were tossed inside the shed. The inside was barren except for a pile of hay on one side and a bucket on the other.

"Bedding and space for relief," Trise pointed to the hay and bucket respectively.

"And food?" Parner asked expectantly.

"Maybe," Trise said, instructing Gertrude to close the door behind them.

They heard the sound of a lock being placed at the door, then a series of footsteps and banter left the area outside the shed.

"Well," Parner said, squirming his was to lay down on the pile of hay, "what now?"

"Why did you have to speak to them so much, Parner? Why is it that you can never shut your mouth?" Aten yelled.

"No, he did well, Roth," Ren said, rolling over to reveal he had already released the bonds of his rope. Aten blinked in surprise. Ren pointed to his ear, then pointed outside. Aten understood immediately. The women might be listening.

"Then what do we do, Boros?" Aten asked, a bittersweet feeling washing over him from remembering his last interaction with Boros.

Ren began undoing the binds on his legs and spoke loudly.

"We wait for them to take us to Berdun, we are their captives after all," he said, a fire in his eyes.

11

Aten rubbed at his wrists, followed by the rest of his bruised body, as Ren had just freed him from his binds. He felt tenderly at his shoulder and winced, then began to pull off the armor around it.

"No," Ren put a hand on top of the armor, preventing it from coming off.

"Please," Aten whispered, pointing to his shoulder.

"We do not know when they will return. We should be prepared for anything," Ren whispered in return.

"But Ren—"

"But *Boros*," Ren corrected, pointing outside.

"My shoulder is flaring up," Aten said.

"Very well, but just the upper part," Ren sighed, moving to Parner and untying the rope on his arms and legs.

"I, for one, am in desperate need to have my thirst quenched," Parner said to the closed door.

Aten felt his throat itch and could not help but nod in agreement. He began fiddling at the straps to the armor connected above his waist. Ren leaned against the door, keeping his ear laid against it.

"Yes, but in the meanwhile, can either of you explain to me why..." Aten paused to think of the fake name they were using for Parner before realizing he was not given one, "...Parner is not being reprimanded for telling the captors everything they wanted to know and more?"

"Everything they wanted to know and more?" Parner repeated, amused. "You sound like a salesman, Roth."

Aten's eyebrows descended an inch before he remembered that his name for the foreseeable future would be "Roth." He felt strange about being assigned his deceased friend's name. He missed him. Roth's death was a constant reminder of the consequences of his actions. Or inaction to kill Vesta sooner.

"Why did you tell them that we had no other supplies? We could have at least feigned that we had others in our party and that we were only scouting ahead?" Aten asked.

"And how long would you suggest we continue that bluff?" Parner asked. Then he widened his eyes and pointed to the opposite end of the shed while smiling, "Ah! There they are, right around the corner! Oh, you just missed them Trise, we will surely escape when they come to see us when you have your back turned," Parner said sarcastically.

"Do not be ridiculous Parner—"

"Oh, ridiculous? Yes, *I* am the one being ridiculous. I did not think to begin a ruse when being dragged and bruised by a dozen captors while still groggily dusting off the sleep I had been enjoying. Roth, when you are held captive, if you begin speaking the truth, then they are bound to accept everything you say as the truth. Think about the women around Trise. Gertrude, was it? She believes there is another dragon after us, as do many of the others in that… female crew of theirs," Parner said, unable to think of a more scathing name.

"What good does that do us? We are still in captivity and still without water," Aten replied. He removed the final strap of the armor and set it to the side. He rolled his bad shoulder slowly, making sure not to move it in a direction it disagreed with. He also took note of his leg, which seemed in surprisingly good shape. The skin, though mutilated and pink, held well together and had none of the throbbing pain flowing through it that his shoulder did.

"They are undoubtedly discussing the authenticity of the truth now," Ren answered aloud, then changed to a whisper. "And with that will come disunity."

"Disunity?" Aten asked curiously.

"Trise seemed a stubborn one," Parner explained, "Likely to stay convinced that the best course of action is to receive a payment and leave the wretches of Berdun to deal with us and the possibility of a dragon. The others, as you may have noticed, feel a bit more inclined to believe us and therefore will want to be rid of us sooner. Who would want to have a dragon hunting down their party, after all? Regardless of the decision made, we may be able to leverage their fears."

Aten absorbed the information with awe. He was fascinated by how Parner put it all together. All he could see was that he was trapped in this wooden prison, but his brethren were already thinking steps ahead.

"So," Aten began, slowly piecing ideas together, "when you continued to bring up the subject of the dragon…"

"It was because they had shown such a strong reaction to it, yes. Controversial topics will always drive a wedge between people, no matter how close they may seem," Parner said.

Aten nodded, agreeing. He felt more confident now, less like prisoners waiting to be taken as slaves and more like a cornered animal preparing its ferocious counterattack.

"What are we to tell them next?" Aten asked.

Ren and Parner looked to one another.

"*We* will play it by ear. You should generally keep quiet," Parner said apologetically.

"Beg your pardon?" Aten asked, flummoxed.

"Roth, you are a brave knight, that I cannot deny. But you…" Parner lowered his voice, "you are too sincere. You would be hard-pressed to tell a lie, much less build upon one. If we resort to that, as we did our names, it is best to allow us to handle it."

"I can deceive foe!" Aten protested.

"Can you? When have you last done that? When have you ever operated in a state of misinformation?" Parner challenged.

Aten looked around the floor, recollecting his experiences. Nothing of note came to mind. Not even when faced with death between the arrow of Tholen and the claws of Vesta did he lie his way out, he only delivered a nonanswer. He looked to his other companion.

"Ren—"

Ren put a hand up sternly. Aten's heart sunk to his stomach when he immediately realized he had not called him 'Boros' again.

"These are admirable traits to have," Ren said reassuringly. "Let us handle instances where you are weak and you will handle that which requires immense bravery."

Aten felt patronized rather than assuaged.

"So I am weak then? It seems I have been nothing but weak for as long as I have known dragons," Aten said sourly.

"But you defeated one!" Ren said, imbuing his words with pride.

"After I watched it slaughter so many. And when I returned home, I fled at the sight of the next dragon. Not on my own two feet, mind you. I was too weak for that as well. I had to be carried, then dragged here. I feel—I *am* weak."

Parner was quick to jump in,

"And yet the dragon searches for you. Whatever you may think of yourself, you are a Dragonslayer. And we—as well as all of Pallas— would not be alive if not for your quick assessment of the situation when the threat arrived at our hometown."

The knot in Aten's stomach loosened.

"What is our plan?" he asked, resolving to bury the conversation at that.

Ren perked up at the door, as if hearing something outside, while Parner closed his eyes in thought. Aten watched the two of them closely, hoping to learn something from their behavior and be useful like them. Ren's face tightened in concentration, then loosened just as suddenly. He nodded that it was safe to continue conversing for the time being.

"We press the issue of the dragon until we are thrown out of their possession for fear of attracting its wrath. Even Roth could join then, for it is nothing short of the truth," Parner suggested.

"Except if they are led by Trise, we should assume we will either be ignored or shut up. Likely the latter considering you are hard to ignore," Ren said.

"Even if we were to manage to be rid of them somehow, we do not even know where we are," Aten said.

"Based on how far we were dragged, and that we were brought North, I would wager that we are on the outskirts of Banti. If we could escape, convince, or overpower our captors, we may be able to find respite or supplies there. Water," Parner said, his eyes still closed.

"Banti? This is a place you are familiar with?" Aten asked hopefully.

"No, I have only seen it on the maps we studied in the guild," Parner admitted.

"Then we do not know whether they will side with these women," Ren said. "For all we know, they could be acting on orders from the town. Even in the case we convince them, we will not be admitted in fear of bringing the dragon there."

Parner nodded in agreement. He sighed.

"And in the case we do end up in Berdun... Have either of you ever fought or killed before?" Parner asked. Suddenly he went red when Aten opened his arms wide. "Err... Killed a fellow man?" he clarified.

"Not I," Aten said. "I have only fought off bandits on the outskirts of Pallas. Only delivered a few shallow cuts, nothing lethal."

"Nor I," Ren shook his head uncomfortably.

"Fantastic. That makes three of us in a ring of killers if we reach Berdun. We may last an entire minute if we use Roth as a meat shield!" Parner said, opening his eyes. "I am afraid I have no plan that strikes me as satisfactory. What about the two of you?"

Aten was surprised he was even offered a chance to give a plan. He gave it a moment's thought.

"Tackle whoever it is that opens the door and hold them hostage," he offered.

"Charging in is not a plan, it is a manifestation of desperation. One that will not be taken kindly," Ren said, sliding a finger across his throat. "It needs to be more thought out than flinging our bodies at them."

"But we are assets, potentially worth a lifetime of a fortune according to them. We even witnessed when Parner mocked them that we are too valuable to damage," Aten protested.

"Maybe when we are bound at the wrist or being dragged through a forest in the dead of night, but not when we are putting up a fight," Parner said, wiggling the rope that was no longer binding his arms together. Aten shrugged. He still thought it a good plan.

Ren looked to the other side of the shed where the bucket lay. He scrunched his face in disgust. He looked to the pile of hay, then back to the door they were led in by.

"I may have an idea, but it is wretched, disgusting, and wicked," Ren offered.

"Three words that aptly describe the very situation we are in, Boros," Parner said with a grin.

"Very well," Ren said, his face turning cold, "this is what I propose…"

12

Aten breathed in deep, measured breaths as he awaited beneath the pile of hay with his brethren. He had fully readorned his armor. His chest went tight as he anticipated the opening of the shed door. Ren heard their captors approaching from the distance and set them in their positions as soon as possible. Sure enough, Gertrude's voice was soon at the other end of the door.

"I am going to need you all to step to the other end of the shed before I open the door," Gertude commanded. "I want to give you some water."

Aten licked his cracked lips. Parner sighed next to Aten, likely just as parched.

"Hello?" Gertrude said, knocking on the door. "I am not going to open this door until you give me an indication that you are on the other side of the building."

Her voice began to quiver toward the end of her sentence.

"Hey!" she punched the door. "I am not in the mood for games!"

Gertrude began fumbling with a set of keys just outside the door. Aten tensed, preparing himself. Ren placed a calming hand down on his arm. They did not want to spring any earlier than they had planned.

"All right, that is it!" Gertrude shrieked. She unlocked the door and kicked it open. A bucket of waste that had been filled with the trio's excreta fell down from above the door. Gertrude gagged in disgust and tumbled backward, falling on her back.

The three sprung from under the hay and darted to the open door. Gertrude flailed around at the sound of their steps and screamed,

"Trise! Trise!"

Aten ran out of the shed first, nimbly jumping over Gertrude and making sure to land on his good foot first. An arrow whizzed past him and he turned to look at Trise who was preparing another arrow and taking aim at Ren and Parner who came out just behind him.

Ren scooped up the pail of water that was next to Gertrude and threw it at Trise, breaking her focus and causing her to dive out of the way.

"I wanted to drink some of that!" Parner complained.

"Now is sincerely not the time!" Ren said.

Immediately outside of the shed, the treeline was only a few dozen feet away. A few more seconds and they would make it free once more.

"We are going to—"

Aten turned around and saw Ren and Parner tripping over a rope and colliding into one another, collapsing to the floor. Aten followed the rope and saw Trise had tied one end to an arrow and let it loose, creating a sort of trip-wire. She was nocking another arrow and aiming at them while they still lay on the floor, recollecting themselves. Aten was disgusted, typical of the archer to attack those who are weak. Aten wheeled his weight around and went charging toward Trise.

"AAAHHH!!" he bellowed, holding one arm high.

Just as he was about to tackle her, she deftly slid to one side and ducked, avoiding both Aten's body and the flail of his arm. While he tried to slow himself down, she kicked him from behind his knee and had him falling face first on the earth. As soon as he caught himself, she pressed her knee against her back and held an arrow at his neck. The two of them panted a few seconds before she spoke,

"Is this escape done?" she called to Ren and Parner who were both sitting on the floor in awe. Gertrude was behind them now, a bow and arrow of her own drawn and pointed at the two of them, though her nose was scrunched and her face awash with revulsion.

"Yes, I would say so," Parner conceded.

"What!?" Aten screamed. He could hear footsteps approaching, likely the rest of the girls that followed Trise.

"Roth, let us—"

Parner's jaw dropped open as his gaze caught sight of something to the East. Aten could not see what he was looking at, but watched as Ren and Gertrude followed Parner's gaze and came to the same expression. Behind him, he heard Trise gasp quietly.

"What? What is it?" Aten asked, trying to stand up. Trise added more weight to her knee and kept him where he was.

"Trise…" Gertrude said slowly.

"Yes, I see it!" Trise snapped.

"If this is not evidence of a dragon, then I think you would prefer to die in ignorance than accept truth!" Parner said to Trise.

"There is no dragon!" she screamed, kicking Aten to the ground.

"What is it?" Aten groaned.

"Nothing!" Trise yelled.

"It is a giant column of smoke a distance to the East, likely another fire caused by the dragon by the size of it," Parner answered him.

"There are many explanations to why there may be smoke rising from the East, a dragon is just one of them!" Trise exploded.

"Oh yes, and other scenarios include a town-wide meal where everyone cooks meat at the same time to broadcast how much food they collectively have!" Parner mocked, smiling.

"Gertrude, shut him up!" Trise said.

"But Trise, what if it is a dragon?" Gertrude asked.

"Shut him up!" she repeated.

"I just want you to think on how often you have seen flames this large, ever in any of the generations of people you know in your life!" Parner ordered.

"Gertrude!"

"Parner, I am going to have to ask you to be quiet for a time," Gertrude relented, pointing her bow at him. Parner smiled and shrugged.

In this time, the other girls in Trise's group had gathered around them, weapons in hand prepared for a fight. Aten turned to look at them and saw that they were collectively staring in the direction of the smoke as well, most squirming or looking uncomfortable. He smirked to himself. Parner was effective.

"Trise, what are we going to do if it is a dragon?" one of them asked quietly. She was the smallest of them, yet wielded a longbow.

Trise sighed impatiently.

"We are still going to bind these fools and send them up the river, Sylva," Trise declared.

Aten saw some of them relax.

"Send them up the river alone, then? Out of our city?" Sylva asked.

"Alone? Do not be foolish, I still intend to sell them off," Trise said plainly.

The girls who relaxed tensed up again.

"Quickly, bind them before they come up with any more pathetic attempts at escape," Trise ordered, tossing a cord of rope at one of them. A few walked around Aten to attend to tying up Ren and Parner. Aten felt his arms tied behind his back followed by his legs. He was finally turned over and allowed to see the spectacle that everyone had been in shock of.

An arm made of black clouds lazily reached into the air etching a scar into the otherwise blue sky. Aten followed it down to the source and found that it could not have been more than a day's travel away. The dragon may still be looking for them, and it was still nearby.

He was then hoisted up by two girls and walked a few paces behind the shed and tossed into a cart. He noticed that his, Parner, and Ren's weapons were stacked on one end of it. One by one Parner and Ren were tossed in after him.

"A cart? Why were we dragged in nets last night if we get a cart now?" Parner asked no one in particular.

"Quiet, Parner," Trise ordered.

"I am flattered you remember my name," Parner smiled.

Trise sighed and moved to the front to pull on the cart along with a half-dozen other girls. Gertrude walked beside the cart, keeping an eye on the three and making sure they remained bound and within the cart.

"No horses," Ren whispered to the others. Aten nodded. A horse may be expensive to maintain, but between the dozen girls and the town nearby, he found it surprising that they did not have one to share. On the other hand, not a single farmer in Pallas had a horse either.

"What do we do now?" Aten asked the knights.

"We do not have much a choice but to let this take its course," Parner said.

"What are you whispering about?" Gertrude asked.

"I am just saying," Parner said quickly, "I do not understand why we were dragged yesterday when we are in the cart today. If we are so valuable, why risk us being torn up by the sharp rocks loose on the earth?"

"What did he say about Torn?" Sylva asked nervously.

"Nothing, he was speaking of something else entirely," Gertrude assured.

"Yes, the Kingdom of Torn is nothing to worry about..." Parner nodded.

Gertrude nodded back to him, appreciating the corroboration.

"...the dragon on the other hand..." Parner said, tilting his head with overexaggerated uncertainty.

"Enough of that!" Trise barked.

The cart was dragged on for what seemed like an hour before Aten heard the sound of running water.

"Can we please get something to drink?" Parner begged genuinely.

"If you had listened to my instructions in the shed, you would not be complaining right now," Gertrude replied.

"Yes, but my throat feels so dry that it might start cracking. Please," Parner said.

Aten looked up at her and nodded in agreement, pleading with his eyes.

"All right, lower them in," Trise said.

"Lower us? You intend to drown us now?" Aten asked. Trise frowned at him and shook her head hopelessly at him.

He was lifted first and placed into a boat on the edge of a river, followed by his comrades. He noticed his weapons were left behind, likely to be used or sold by whoever remained ashore.

"Give them some water now, so they can shut up about it," Trise said.

Gertrude grabbed a pail from the cart and filled it, then splashed it on herself, washing herself of filth before quenching the thirst of those who attacked her. A few minutes of cleaning later, she held the same bucket filled with water at the lips of each of them who drank heartily. Aten never felt so soothed as he was by the blessing of water in his aching throat. He felt revitalized in places he had not realized were fatigued.

"We are to go up the river, then?" Ren asked.

"Yes, Berdun is not far ahead by boat," Trise nodded.

Aten squinted at the river, followed by the path beyond it. He continued following this path until he ended up staring straight into the sky.

"Are my eyes playing tricks, or are we heading straight in the direction of the column of smoke?" Aten asked.

13

The traveling crew was split between two boats, one with Trise, Gertrude, and the three knights, and the other with a half-dozen girls, which included Sylva. Trise had silenced everyone and ordered no one speak until they reached Berdun, but that did not stop them from pulling at their clothes or tugging nervously at their bowstrings. Aten disliked that their nerves led them to their bow and turned to look up.

Aten watched the sky in awe, the light of the sun being overpowered by the sheer magnitude of the cloud of soot drifting lazily above them. He could stare at the sun without pain reaching his eyes. Every time he followed it down to the base, he was certain that they were heading in that direction, but said nothing more about it. He did not wish to have his injuries increased by any means and was in no mood to test Trise's patience by asking about it again.

Gertude murmured to herself faintly while she steered the boat along the river. The boat rocked gently with her movements, causing Aten to feel a sense of calm. Gertrude kept trying to make eye contact with Trise, whose steely gaze remained locked forward on their destination. Around the fifth time Gertrude looked her way, Trise sighed and leaned over to Aten.

"Roth, what do you know of Vesta?" she asked.

Aten stared at her for a moment before remembering that he was still going by Roth.

"I know that she is dead?" Aten offered.

"No, I mean... how am I to believe you bested Vesta if you know nothing of her?" she asked.

Aten raised an eyebrow. It seemed Trise was coming around to the idea of the dragon being at Berdun after all.

"Vesta was proud, but not arrogant. She dressed regally, as though a part of royalty, and had a lair that would induce nightmares in even the most weathered fighters. Her home was a moat of death, layer upon layer of dead men's bones lined a rich horde of treasure. She was indiscernible from a woman like yourself, except that she had wings sprouting from her back and narrower pupils," Aten explained.

Trise frowned distastefully at the description.

"I am sure Vesta has a lot more differences from me than just the wings," she said.

"Perhaps," Aten shrugged.

"Yes," Parner jumped in, pulling on his restraints mischievously, "if she were alive perhaps we would be able to compare the two of you, but as it stands, you sound just as bad as Vesta."

Gertrude shook her head to Parner as Trise turned and kicked the wind out of him. The boat rocked violently and the girls aboard the other boat craned their necks to see what was happening on their leader's boat. Aten and Ren stared, but knew Parner would have to deal with the consequences of his actions on his own.

"My God," Parner coughed, managing a slight grin through his grimace, "I was speaking in jest."

"I do not jest about the monster who killed my father," Trise snarled.

Parner looked up, stunned, all semblance of humor fled from his face.

"I... I did not know, I..." Parner said, lowering his head in shame.

Trise looked back out to the smoke the river was leading them to.

"Tell me how you managed to kill Vesta," she spoke to Aten.

Aten looked to Ren, ensuring he was intended to reveal this much information. Ren nodded encouragingly.

"I learned that a dragon's weakness is to strike its vulnerable heart. I did just that, and she fell," Aten recounted.

"And not only did the entirety of Pallas and Banti not strike her heart, but somehow you were able to manage it? And not only did she perish, but her father now seeks revenge? How am I to believe that?" Trise asked angrily.

"Only if you wish to believe the truth," Ren said.

She glared at him, then closed her eyes and rubbed her temples.

"Your father fought Vesta?" Aten asked, curious.

Trise continued to rub her temples in silence. Gerturde cleared her throat and answered for her,

"Banti was approached by an old man that came from Pallas years ago, perhaps seven or eight years. Elder Anderros?"

"Anderson?" Aten clarified.

"That is he. He bartered with Banti during a very hard time. The harshest winter in memory. He asked that we send our able-bodied men to clear a creature from the forest neighboring Pallas and we would be paid with half of Pallas's harvest for that fall. Half! We could live years on that amount of food. We agreed, all the men of our village went off to fight and give their families something to hope for in the coming winter.

"We never learned exactly what happened to them. No doubt, Vesta was the one that took them down, but we never were delivered any news that they had fallen in battle, nor were we ever paid for the loss of their lives. We waited for a month's time before going to Pallas to extract the news ourselves. Simply told that they were dead, with a shrug at that."

"But you were then paid the yield for the job done?" Aten asked.

"Anderson told us that the deal was to kill Vesta, and she lived on in her cave. Without our side of the bargain filled, he said Pallas was absolved of any agreements we made," Gertrude shrugged.

Aten looked back to Trise. Her jaw was locked tight, and she was shaking slightly. Her father was another casualty of Vesta's. Another reason Aten was right in Vesta having to die. But the consequences of her death felt so much larger than any inaction would have caused. The new dragon burned down his home, killed his brethren, and drove him into the arms of slavers.

"How many men remained in Banti?" Aten asked Gertrude. Trise shook her head and spoke,

"Any that remained in Banti were weak and died in the course of that winter. We were forced to take matters in our own hands and became bandits to provide for the people of our town."

"How noble of you to go into slave trading to save your village," Parner mocked.

"You may be leading your people into more danger," Ren warned, pointing to the sky with his chin.

"Yes, Trise, let us be rid of the three of them!" Gertrude pleaded. "Toss them overboard and let us return to Banti where it is safe!"

"Gertrude, I will hear none of it. We have come this far, let us be paid for our work," Trise replied simply.

"Paid by whom?" Parner asked.

"Shut up, Parner," Trise warned.

"You have discovered three refugees from Pallas and decide to go headfirst into what they warn will also make you refugees? Or worse?" Ren asked.

Aten realized that Parner and Ren were following the plan to divide the women, and it seemed to be working.

"Trise, what if they speak the truth?" Sylva asked from the other boat nervously.

"When have our prisoners ever spoken the truth? They have told any number of lies to be free of us before we reached Berdun because they are afraid!" Trise yelled back to her.

"I am afraid," Parner agreed, "of the dragon."

"As am I," Ren nodded.

"Err... yes, me as well," Aten nodded. In truth, he did not fear Vesta's father, but he wanted to join Parner and Ren. Ren shook his head almost imperceptibly at him.

"You see how Roth speaks hesitantly, as though waiting for the right time to speak, this is how they have determined to manipulate us! They are intelligent, but they are still liars!" Trise said.

Aten's heart fell to his stomach when he saw a few girls nodding to that logic. He truly was very poor at deceiving an enemy.

"Liars that came up with a way to burn down Berdun?" Parner said without missing a beat.

"Quiet, Parner, Berdun is fine, I am sure the fire started beyond their lands," Trise said.

"Trise, I ask that we at least hear out the capabilities of a dragon before we head into the flames!" Gertrude said.

"Gertrude, they will just lie in whatever way will make it easiest for them to escape their sale. Hold out for less than one more hour and we can be done with them!" Trise screamed.

"One hour is more than enough for the dragon to kill us," Ren shrugged.

"Boros could not have made my point any more clear, see?" Trise pointed to Ren.

"Or maybe he was—"

"I will not—"

Trise began to cough as the overpowering smell of ash filled the air. She looked up and absorbed the sheer pervasiveness the smoke had on the sky now. The sun was shrouded and cast a red glare over the land. She looked at her crew seriously.

"Stealth," she ordered, her voice level.

Without protest, each girl nodded and ducked down silently, making the boats look as though they were empty and drifting aimlessly on the river.

"What are we—"

"Parner, no more games. If you speak one more word, I will carve your tongue out," Trise whispered, placing the head of an arrow at his cheek. Parner swallowed and nodded.

For a few minutes, the boats drifted steadily, the loudest noise was the sound of the water flowing around them. Aten began thinking that his heartbeat alone would be enough to attract the dragon. It was thundering within him, preparing for another encounter with the beast that destroyed his home. He breathed slowly, controlling his nerves. Even if he was to die here, he would attempt to strike at the dragon's heart.

Suddenly, with enough force to make Ren jump in fright, Gertrude gasped and placed a hand over her mouth.

Berdun was in view. A giant pile of ashes, with more falling from the sky. There was not an intact structure in sight. The remains of the city were a ghastly mix of black and dark red, the remnants of what must have been the inhabitants of the town. Etched in the ground were outlines of those blasted by the direct fire from the dragon, presumably. Aten sat up and absorbed the scene somberly. Another action committed as a consequence for Vesta's death. Aten felt at this rate he would wish Vesta was back tormenting Pallas alone rather than her father taking down the entirety of the Kingdom of Kolog.

For a few minutes, the boats drifted away as none of the ones meant to steer the boat could pry their eyes away from the scene. Never had any one of them seen such destruction take place to any land before. It was carnage on scales they had never imagined possible.

"Take us in," Trise ordered.

They numbly followed the command, bringing them to the riverbank. The girls began filing out, looking in each direction searching for some explanation. Aten got up and hopped out of the boat as well, to which no one seemed bothered. Even Aten did not think to escape after witnessing Berdun. What first was a town that he dreaded he would have to kill another man within, he now feared he would not find another living being.

"There are hardly any signs of a struggle, or any tracks indicating anyone came or left the area," Parner said seriously, hopping out of the boat after Aten.

"And?" Trise asked.

"It was senseless killing. It was the dragon," he said, frowning.

"There is no dragon," Trise said softly, but this time monotonously as if she was so used to saying the sentence that she could not help but say it even if she may not have believed herself as much anymore.

Aten saw that Ren remained on the boat and had tears flowing down his eyes. Aten wondered why he himself did not have the same reaction to witnessing something so harrowing.

"Alive!" Sylva screamed next to the ashes of what may have been the arena.

"What?" Trise asked, running over followed by the rest of them. Aten hopped over in his bindings, determined to see anything that could have survived.

Aten was finally able to catch up and see Sylva holding someone up gingerly by the back of their head and pouring a light stream of water into his mouth. He was covered in soot from head to toe and looked as though he was a man made of coal, except for the bloodshot eyes, wide in their sockets. He was shivering and his eyes were unable to focus on anything or anyone, just darting around in fear and pain.

"What happened to you?" Trise asked him. The crowd leaned in.

The man's eyes continued to flail around the sky until his gaze landed upon Aten and he coughed, then spoke.

"A—Apoph—Apo—"

He coughed again, slumped into Sylva's hand, then passed away.

14

The small band of warrior women and knights stared at the body in Sylva's arms in shock. Sylva gently placed the man's head on the ground and Gertrude turned to throw up in the river. Aten's body was completely devoid of feeling having watched the man's soul leave him. Sylva slid her hand across his face and closed his eyes.

"We will bury him?" Sylva turned up to look at Trise.

"Yes," Trise nodded, then looked around, "as well as the rest of the bodies that we can find. A grave for each of them."

The girls began to look around for something to dig with, none of them complaining despite the fact it may take hours, even the full day to bury all of the bodies of those intact. Aten watched them, still bound and unable to help, despite the fact he would. He turned to Parner who was standing looking up at the soot in the sky, uncharacteristically quiet. Parner hopped over to him and sighed.

"I am…sorry Aten. I fought you when you determined the best course of action was to track the dragon and defeat it. I told you it would probably leave us all well alone. I was a fool, and I apologize for any frustration my foolishness caused you," he said sincerely.

Aten nodded and bumped him with his elbow, unable to show any other form of comradery while still in ropes.

"Whether you agreed with me or not, we could not have stopped this from happening. I appreciate your words, Parner. It takes a valiant knight to admit he was wrong, and willingly so," Aten said.

The moment he said the words, the thought passed through his head: Was he wrong to have killed Vesta? Was he just too stubborn to admit it? No, she killed the innocent girl Didra, her father, and the men of the village of Banti. Vesta's father was clearly a monster and she likely had the same evil within her. It was inevitable.

"Rest assured, Aten. I will do everything in my power to assist you in defeating this dragon," Parner promised. Aten nodded graciously.

Gertrude came back from the river, wiping her mouth with her forearm. Trise approached the two knights, frowning.

"Who said anything about a dragon? The man was going to say a pack of bandits, no?" Trise asked.

Gertrude's face went red with rage and she stomped toward the three of them and stood in the face of Trise.

"This was not the work of a pack of bandits! Clearly this was a dragon!" she screamed.

The girls gathering bodies stopped and looked up.

"Then why did the man not say that? A simple word? He was trying to say a phrase, like a pack of something!" Trise retorted.

"He was trying to say a dragon, but as death overcame his conscious, so did delirium! He was in desperate need of water and could hardly make out sounds! He did not know what he was saying, but only a fool would believe this town was brought to ash by a petty pack of bandits!" Gertrude yelled.

The girls came bounding over from their various spots in town. Aten watched Trise and Gertrude carefully. While they squabbled before, it seemed even the young women under their command were surprised to see them fighting in this manner.

"Did you call me a fool?" Trise asked, venom in her words.

"If you sincerely believe that the town of gladiators could be brought down by bandits that do not leave as much as a set of footprints behind, then I can not think of you than any less than a fool," Gertrude swore.

Aten saw Parner watching passively. This was the culmination of the division he spoke of earlier, but it seemed that their goading did little to spark this flame of confrontation.

"Gertrude, I am warning you," Trise began, but even she looked unsettled by Gertrude's ferocity.

"Trise. Turn around. Look at Berdun. Do you remember being able to see that forest from the river? The one that would eventually lead you to Kolog Bay?" she asked, pointing a stern finger.

Trise turned to look, but did not answer.

"Everything is gone. Obliterated. Without a shred of an explanation past what we have been told by these knights. A dragon roams this land. It burned down Pallas, then continued and burned down Berdun," Gertrude said.

Trise looked at the ground trying to think of something to say.

"No," she whispered.

"It is the only way to make sense of this," Gertrude urged.

"But…"

"Trise look there! Remember that building! It's where the fisherman lived, Drake. Do you remember his daughters, how much they loved when you came to visit?" Gertrude asked, pointing to the smoldering remains of a building. Trise stared numbly. "What do you think happened to them? You think it was bandits?"

Trise did not reply.

"And there," Gertrude continued, pointing another direction. "That was the weaponsmith, Rinald. We used to buy arrows from there whenever we came by. Do you think Rinald would be defeated by bandits? The man was twice our size! Do you see a single stray arrow or weapon on the earth? Do you still believe it was bandits?"

Trise suddenly closed her eyes, a tear falling freely,

"I want you to remember Berdun. The men in armor at all hours of the day and the women and children who had such purpose that they only had determination in their eyes. Think, Trise! Would a simple pack of bandits be enough to snuff out the life here?! Think!" Gertrude urged.

Trise opened her eyes once more, her gaze distant, looking at each of the ashes that served as remains of the city. She thought of the shopkeepers she considered allies and the children she would play with. She wiped her eyes sullenly. Then, took on fiery determination and stood tense, looking around. She eyed Aten for a second, then began firing off orders,

"Gather this town's supplies. While most of their belongings may be gone, I am willing to bet their gold, silver, and bronze coins were able to withstand the attack. Check every body before burying it. And free the knights from their binds. Without Berdun, they are little more than worthless to us. We may be hit next by an attack from the dragon and we must gather all the supplies we can in case we must flee Banti!"

"But Trise," Sylva protested, "how do we know the knights will not attack us once we free them?"

Trise patted her bow lightly,

"The consequences would be far too dire. Furthermore, we are not their enemy, the dragon is. Correct?" she turned to Parner and Aten.

"That is right," Parner nodded eagerly. Aten did not respond, narrowing his eyes at Trise and her bow. He did not trust her.

"Move as quickly as possible, we want to be back in Banti tomorrow at the latest," Trise said, then turned to Gertrude. "I am sorry for being stubborn. You were right, I was a fool."

Gertrude looked ashamed.

"I am sorry for undermining you in front of the others," she said.

"Better to be humiliated than to be a blind leader," Trise reassured.

The two of them joined the others in gathering supplies and taking bodies to one side of the city to create graves. Before they were left alone, Parner and Aten's binds were cut off by Sylva who eyed them warily.

"Who knew the dragon would bring us the blessing of freedom?" Parner said, rubbing at his wrists.

Aten furled his eyebrows.

"Yes, I regretted it as soon as I said it," Parner said sheepishly, looking to what used to be a town full of life.

They went over to the river and greeted Ren who still sat dejectedly in the boat, staring into the river sullenly.

"We are free," Aten said, trying to snap him out of his trance.

Ren shrugged slightly. Parner approached him and began untying his binds. Ren was despondent.

"Ren?" Aten said, getting into the boat and sitting in front of him.

"How long until you think the dragon reaches Kit?" Ren asked, his voice shaky.

"What?" Parner said, surprised.

"Our people fled Pallas and went to Kit. How long until they are given the same treatment that Berdun was delivered?" Ren asked.

Aten and Parner looked to one another for answers neither had.

"We must consider the positives here Boros," Parner said slowly, "We are free and the people of Pallas are safe!"

"Not all the people of Pallas. Anderson, Unis, all of the knights guild, all dead. The entire city of Berdun. The dragon came back from its heading eastward. It will reach Kit," Ren said, his lip trembling.

"Unless we stop it," Aten said confidently.

"You still think you can face it? A creature so fast, it went far beyond a full day's travel in a matter of minutes. So powerful, not even the Royal Guard of the North could defeat its daughter, and so angry that it burned down Pallas and Berdun out of spite!" Ren sighed in disbelief, running a hand through his hair.

"We just need to visit Pirulo. He was able to teach me how to defeat Vesta. I am certain he will have the key to stopping her father," Aten assured him.

"How do we know Pirulo is that wise? Or even alive for that matter?" Ren said, finally looking up to Aten, his eyes glistening in fresh tears.

"I promise you that Pirulo is wise. He was safeguarded by the Deserted Desert itself in a beautiful and bountiful oasis, he will be alive and well," Aten promised.

Ren closed his eyes and breathed a long breath out his nose. He stood up slowly and wiped his eyes.

"Very well, Roth. I do not wish to die, but I will join the suicide mission," Ren said reluctantly.

Aten nodded with respect. He was honored to have his brothers with him to the end on his journey, and he was glad to not be alone in confronting a dragon again. He needed people he trusted around him to ensure he did what was right, and he trusted his fellow knights with his life.

"If it is true that we are free, I suppose we no longer need to maintain the fake identities," Ren suggested.

"No," Aten said quickly, turning to look at the young archer women. "I do not believe that would be wise to do, yet."

Parner and Ren seemed confused, but nodded regardless.

"Parner," Aten began, "do you know how we could get to the Deserted Desert the fastest from this location? Will the river take us there?"

Parner shut his eyes in thought. He drew a map in the air and mumbled to himself as he cut through the imaginary map in a dozen different places.

"Yes, this river will lead us to the desert. If I remember the maps we studied correctly, it should lead us to Sekoa, which I believe lies on the eastern edge of the desert. Would that be sufficient?" Parner asked.

"It is a start," Aten nodded. "Ren—Boros, do you know how best to travel up rivers, considering where to stop for the night and how to maintain a consistent speed in the day?"

Ren shrugged, saying,

"I hope you enjoy eating fish for days on end."

Aten smiled, then jumped when he saw that Gertrude was standing not more than a few paces away from them. She was looking over her shoulder nervously. Aten glared and asked her,

"What do you want?"

"To give you this," she said, rushing forward and dropping a small pile of bronze and silver coins into Ren's hand. Ren looked up shocked.

Aten felt a rock form in his gut. He could not help but feel like he did the first time he confronted Vesta. Vesta had given him a treasure, spoils from someone she killed and this felt no different, especially considering it was her father that killed the people that brought this bounty.

"What is this?" Aten asked, offended.

"Take it and leave, I want us to have nothing to do with you. Take a boat, too, while no one watches. Take the dragon that chases you along as well," Gertrude said hurriedly, peeking over her shoulder once again. She went tense when Trise began coming her way.

"We do not want your money," Aten spat.

"Right, except that we do," Parner corrected, taking some of the coins in Ren's hand and pocketing it.

"Parner, I would not be so desperate as to be beholden to the women who were our captors not an hour ago," Aten argued.

"Please, leave now," Gertrude whispered as Trise drew near.

"We cannot deny that we will be in need of supply when we travel down the river south to Sekoa. I do not even believe there are cities along the way, we will have to make do with whatever traveling merchants or stands we can find!" Parner explained.

"And I would prefer to live on nothing than to take their handouts," Aten said.

"Do you hear yourself? You claim to want to stop at nothing to defeat the dragon, but refuse the first advantage that is brought to our hands?" Parner asked.

"You intend on traveling South from here?" Trise asked.

Aten stopped talking and frowned at being interrupted.

"Yes," Parner nodded, "we wish to reach the Sekoa. I recall a map that showed that the river flowed from here to the lake neighboring it."

"That may be, but that would take you through a series of rapids. You would likely perish in the flow of water," Trise said.

"Then we will walk when we reach the rapids," Aten said curtly.

"Or you could go North," Trise offered.

Parner blinked, and closed his eyes to bring up his mental map.

"North?" he asked.

"You would enter Rowa Lake, head South to Dervin and be taken by the flow of the river all the way to Sekoa in a fraction of the time with half the treachery," Trise said.

"Hmmm," Parner thought.

"You are suggesting they take a boat?" Gertrude asked curiously.

"Yes, it will make sure we arrive as fast as humanly possible," Trise nodded.

"We?" Gertrude said surprised.

"*We?*" Aten asked with disgust.

"Ah, yes, I suppose we could go North first and come around South," Parner nodded, opening his eyes to the intense stares of Aten, Trise and Gertrude. He went red, embarrassed in confusion. "Oh, did I say something foolish?"

"Trise implied that she would join us to Sekoa," Aten growled.

"Implied? I stated a direct fact. I am coming with you to Sekoa, and further to face the dragon," Trise said firmly.

"Oh, excellent," Parner nodded excitedly.

"Trise we cannot go with them!" Gertrude protested.

"That is right," Aten agreed.

"We are not going with them, just me alone," Trise said.

"But you cannot—"

"How dare you—"

"Enough!" Ren shouted irritably. The four turned to him, stunned. "Trise and Gertrude, go speak over there. We will confer in private as well. Come back when you have had your conversation."

"There is no need," Trise said, looking pointedly at Gertrude as she opened her mouth to protest once more.

"*Now,*" Ren ordered.

Trise eyed him, but swiftly pulled Gertrude aside to speak.

"We are not letting her join us," Aten declared as soon as he determined they were out of earshot.

"Let us first consider—"

"Let us first consider that she captured us and was determined to sell us without any regard for our lives, is as stubborn as a fatigued horse on a hot day, and is an archer!" Aten said sternly.

"She knew how best to reach the desert! Think about how dire the consequences may have been if we were left to fare those rapids on our own," Parner said thoughtfully.

"And think of how dire the consequences might have been if we had been sold here just one day before the dragon arrived!" Aten said. "Why are we even contemplating this? What reason do we have to trust her?"

"Her constitution has changed," Ren answered simply.

"Her…"

Aten turned to look at Trise again and took in the differences in her stance. She was shaking just as she did when she spoke of her father's death, and she waved the others under her command over with her hands rather than screaming for them. Aten could not place how she had changed, but Ren was right.

"What difference does that make?" Aten asked.

"She wishes to join us for the same reason we are here, Aten. She seeks revenge. Just as we want vengeance for the loss of Pallas and those who fought for it. Revenge for her father through the death of Vesta's. It looks to be why she wants to join us alone, she recognizes this to be a dangerous trek and wants only her life in danger," Ren pointed out.

"That may be..." Aten said, then took a moment to mull over his words. "That may be, but I simply cannot trust her."

The girls began to raise their voices at one another. The entire group had come together to argue over the point of Trise leaving. Sylva threw her arms in the air then stabbed a finger at the knights.

"Trise would be an asset," Parner said, watching her converse with her subordinates. "And if we want to take either of these boats, I am doubtful that we may take it without their permission. Trise would be our sure way to receive that."

Aten looked at Ren, then Parner. They seemed to believe this would be a good idea despite his protests. He did not want to be like Trise and stubbornly go against their wishes. But he also did not trust the archer. He bit the inside of his lip and relented,

"Very well, we will bring Trise along against my better judgements."

"I think that is wise," Ren said.

Parner nodded excitedly, showing the hint of a smile and immediately suppressing it.

The young women spent the next few minutes gesticulating and shaking their head at one another in frustration during which Aten seriously considered taking a boat and leaving while they had the chance. He thought better, especially after agreeing to bring along Trise. Trise was in control of the conversation despite the dozen or so others speaking over one another to get their points across. Then, Gertrude said something and Trise laughed, followed by more discussion. Finally, after the last of Sylva's protests, Gertrude and Trise both came back to the boat.

"We… We would be happy to come with you if you would take us," Gertrude said politely. Trise smirked at her.

"We are coming with you, whether it pleases you or not," Trise clarified.

"The both of you?" Aten asked, newly offended.

"That is right. Either you lose time going on foot and we will follow you anyway, or you agree and take the two of us on our boat," Trise stated.

An awkward moment of thought passed as Aten considered the options with the new addition to the deal.

"Glad to have you along!" Parner announced, looking at Aten. Aten shrugged noncommittally. He had defeated a dragon before. He thought well of his chances dealing with the two archers in case the need arose.

15

Ren stood patiently at the end of the boat, ready to push them off as soon as Trise and Gertrude had said their goodbyes. Aten sat on the opposite end from Trise and Gertrude with his arms crossed, looking out to the river. Sylva and the others were turning their heads between their departing friends as they gave directions.

"Be sure to give them all a proper burial, but not before collecting their valuables," Trise told them.

"Take care of yourselves," Gertrude said.

"If anyone stops you on the way back, you have my permission to kill them," Trise continued.

"Make sure to look out for one another and ration your supplies for the hard times that may be coming ahead," Gertrude told them.

"Do not hesitate to tell the merchants to the north of our new law, but do not leave the village unguarded," Trise said.

"It may be best to unarm the traps surrounding the village," Gertrude suggested.

"Do not disarm any traps. If there are those that wish to raid Banti, let them know that it is still well-guarded even without my being there," Trise ordered.

Gertrude shrugged in agreement.

The women took a moment to look over one another. Sylva sighed.

"You are certain you want to go with… them?" she asked.

Trise looked over her shoulder at Aten and Parner, the former scoffed and the latter smiled amiably.

"We can handle ourselves," she said to Sylva confidently.

Sylva did not look convinced, but Trise signaled Ren to push them off the bank and up the river. The water swept them up immediately, taking them toward Lake Rowa. Trise waved once and turned to look north while Gertrude sang out heartfelt goodbyes to the women they left ashore. As soon as they were out of view, she and Trise immediately picked up oars and began rowing their way North to Arlo.

Aten watched the water intently as they floated down the river, making sure to be turned away from the archers. He did not want to look at them. Through the corner of his eye, he could see Parner trying to think of something to say, and Ren began fiddling with things in the boat to fashion a fishing line.

"Would you like me to row instead?" Parner offered.

"No," Trise replied.

Ren tied a string around a pole that was brought along in the boat and looked around for some form of bait. Gertrude pointed out a box in between rows with her chin. He meticulously tied a worm to a string and tossed it into the water to troll behind the boat, watching the river patiently. Parner wrung his hands.

"What if we were to grab some larger sticks from ashore and row along with you?" Parner suggested.

"No," Trise said simply.

Aten smirked despite himself. Parner was uncomfortable with silence and Trise was already primed to shut down any conversation he tried to strike up. Gertrude glanced at him sympathetically, but continued rowing. Parner opened his mouth, closed it, then opened it again and asked,

"How long until we are in Arlo?"

"Not long," Trise answered.

Aten chuckled, then frowned at himself. He suspected Trise was trying to get on his good side so soon after keeping him and his brothers hostage. Though, having someone who could manage Parner would be an added benefit. Parner sighed and leaned back. He stared at the sky for a few minutes. Aten relished the silence, trying to think of how best to defeat the dragon if it was to approach them now. Would they be able to use the water to their advantage? What had Vesta taught him about dragons in the short time he knew her?

He saw an image of Vesta dying flash in his mind and he shook the idea away. He did not wish to make guesses regarding dragons. It could lead to consequences worse than Vesta's death had caused. Instead, he tried to focus on what "Apoh" might mean, the words the man said before perishing.

Suddenly, an epiphany came to Parner in the form of a nod of his head and he leaned toward Aten.

"Perhaps now is the time to tell them your true names?" Parner whispered.

"What? No! Circumstances have hardly altered since our last conversation regarding this," Aten retorted quietly. He noticed Trise's ear had picked up when she heard them whispering. He leaned closer to Parner.

"They were not our allies before," Parner said.

"They are not our allies now," Aten replied.

"Surely you do not believe them to be our enemies even now? Look how they take on the labor of rowing us upstream while we lounge and converse."

"Yes, but their labor does not equate to trust," Aten said.

"I trust them," Parner said, looking past him at Trise.

"I sincerely cannot imagine why. They dragged you through a forest, threw you in a shed, deprived you of water, intended on selling you to slavery, and even kicked you on the way here," Aten listed, growing more incredulous as each fact came to mind.

"I trust them," Parner shrugged. "I do not believe they would have anything to gain by being our enemies. People are determined by their desires. They desire to see the dragon brought down, just as we do. Our goals align, therefore we should align as well."

"How do you know they do not intend to sell us off to Arlo?" Aten asked.

"A bit ridiculous of a plan to leave the rest of their people behind to do that. They have given us transport and funds for this journey. Should we not be grateful?"

"This is hardly recompense for having held us in captivity," Aten frowned.

"Maybe, but I find it interesting that you are not impressed by their actions despite them not needing to grant us anything. You seemed more trusting even to Vesta," Parner said.

Aten did not have anything to say to that. It was true that he was not impressed and once confronted with the idea he began to wonder why that could be the case. Did he dislike them so much as to throw out any merit they granted? Perhaps it was justified. He felt strange as the only one uncomfortable by their having held them as prisoners and using bows against them when they attempted to flee. Perhaps Ren and Parner see their actions as them carrying out a duty to Banti. But Aten detested the idea of enslaving passersby to Banti regardless of the circumstances.

"I will not say anything of your names without your permission, but I encourage you to tell them sooner rather than later. It will only erode trust the longer it remains under wraps," Parner warned.

Ren perked up and snatched the rod as it began bobbing sharply toward the water. He gave it a massive heave and pulled a fish from the liquid surface. Aten watched in awe as it breached the river, then was disappointed to see the fish flying high enough to clear the boat. Ren tisked as it began arching back down toward the water.

Suddenly, something slapped the fish into the bed of the boat. An oar. Trise used it as a bat to slam it in the air. Hardly giving the fish a glance, she went back to rowing the boat. Ren pounced on it and quickly stabbed it with an arrow given to him by Gertrude.

"Incredible!" Parner said in awe. "How were you able to judge where it would be in the air in such a short amount of time?"

"Over my years with the bow, I have become accustomed to determining the distance to my targets," Trise replied.

"But even then," Ren spoke while gutting the fish, "hitting such a small moving target with something I would not even classify as a weapon is… astounding!"

"Trise likes to make things look easy," Gertrude said. "In truth, she got lucky."

Trise smirked.

"By God!" Parner laughed, "She has a sense of humor! Do you think she can teach you how to find one?" he nudged Ren.

Gertrude laughed as Ren pushed Parner back.

"Perhaps if you gave others more opportunities to speak, you might find out much more about them," Ren smiled.

"Oh ho! How apt an analysis! Did you come up with that as you were brooding in silence for hours on end?" Parner laughed.

"Everyone, be silent," Aten snapped, waving his hands at them.

The four others looked surprised. Gertrude frowned and Trise shook her head disappointedly, looking back to the river. Parner sighed, resigned.

"Roth, we were only—"

"No, I apologize, I did not mean to be rude, but I hear something," Aten said apologetically, picking his head up.

Trise and Gertrude picked up their oars to hear better without the splashing of their rowing. The five drifted slowly as they listened intently for a faint noise at the distance.

"An… an instrument?" Ren asked.

"A lute," Trise said.

"You are certain? A lute?" Aten asked, excited. That was the instrument Pirulo played. Perhaps the bard of old was here.

"We must be near Arlo," Gertrude said, beginning to row again. "We often hear the town before we see it. It sounds like a bard is in the area."

"A bard!" Aten exclaimed eagerly.

"A bit excitable, is he?" Trise asked, amused.

"We are in search of a bard," Parner explained.

"Oh?" Trise asked.

"A bard of old," Aten said, standing to try and get a better view and see the bard. His gaze was met only with trees on the bank, he still could not see any signs of the city. "I met one who taught me how to defeat Vesta when I first spoke to him."

"He taught *you* in particular to slay a dragon?" she asked skeptically.

"He did," Aten nodded, craning his neck and losing his balance on the bobbing boat.

"Why would he withhold the information from the dozens—hundreds of others that went to fight that monster?" she asked bitterly.

Aten looked at her, his lips twitched irritably.

"I do not know, but do not speak of Pirulo as if he does not care for others. He is a wise man who granted me knowledge and respite at no cost. He is not so easily available. That is why we seek Sekoa," Aten said.

"A man who makes it difficult to seek crucial knowledge is no better than one who withholds life or death information. They are both killers," Trise said with distaste.

Aten glared at her.

"Trise!" Gertrude protested.

"Is that the Arlo?" Ren blurted, pointing to the slightest visibility of a port at one end of the river. He looked quickly between Trise and Aten nervously. He sighed in relief when neither were staring down at each other, but instead redirected their attention to the town, now in view.

Arlo had a modest port to a massive town. Aten had never seen a city so large before. The docks were small, fitting ships and boats that could hold no more than twenty people total, with only about a dozen places to tie a boat. In contrast, the buildings nearest to the water were about twice the size of the docks, towering over Aten and his companions. The city was sprawling with life, with over a hundred people visible within the city's bazaar in the town square. Aten had never seen so many people in one place. But even with all these new sights and sounds, the lute still sang high above the cacophony of the crowd. Aten's eyes scanned the people hungrily.

"Take us in," Aten ordered.

Trise rolled her eyes.

"Yes, we were already going to— "

"Does anyone see the bard?" Aten asked.

The others gave cursory glances to the crowd.

"I have an idea," Parner said, patting the coins in his pocket. "Gertrude and Re—Boros can go with Roth to find the bard. Trise and I can gather needed supplies for the trek to Sekoa."

Ren raised an eyebrow at him. Parner forced an innocent smile.

"We need swords since our confiscated goods were left in Banti. And we do not want him traveling alone," Parner suggested, gesturing to Aten who had not looked away from the crowd or acknowledged that he heard Parner at all.

"That may be, but I am staying with Trise," Gertrude said. "Send Roth and Boros together."

Parner frowned, then quickly hid his displeasure and shrugged nonchalantly.

"Very well," Ren nodded.

As soon as the boat was in range, Aten lept from the boat and then winced on the dock, stopping for a moment to assuage the surge of pain running through his bad leg. He had forgotten about the injury in the time he was sitting in the boat. He looked up and was met by the annoyed gaze of a tall woman holding a parchment in hand.

"Hold it, *knight,*" she ordered, looking him up and down.

"Please, I am in a hurry," Aten said rapidly and stepped aside. She stepped in his way.

"I am in charge of the goings and comings of this great town's port. You want to be exiled before you even step foot inside?" she asked, raising an eyebrow and tilting her head to a collection of armed guards playing cards further up the port. Aten noticed how clean the port was, likely maintained by this woman. He also noticed a round scorch mark near where the knights sat. Too small to be part of the dragon's massacre the past days, but nonetheless it made him uneasy. He did not like to be reminded of the dragon's power of fire.

Ren caught up to Aten.

"Our apologies, we did not mean any disrespect, we are just traveling through to Sekoa and are in need of supplies," Ren said cordially. She raised her nose an inch, satisfied.

"Knights, are you?" she asked.

"The men among us are," Ren nodded.

"I am going to need your names," she said, taking a look at her parchment.

"Of course, I am Boros and this is Roth," Ren said, then turned to point to the three on the boat, "and with us are Trise, G—"

"Just the knights," the woman snapped.

"Err, right. Boros, Roth and Parner," Ren said confused.

She grunted.

"And where are you from?" she asked.

Ren hesitated. Aten was unsure of whether they should be sharing that their hometown was burnt down only days ago and cause a panic. Gertrude seemed to read the situation quickly.

"Banti," she answered.

The woman nodded, dissatisfied and put the parchment away.

"You will keep this one out of trouble?" she asked Ren, pointing to Aten.

"Of course," Ren nodded.

"Very well, welcome to Arlo. It will cost you two silver pieces to leave your boat at our dock," she said, holding a hand with the palm up in Aten's face. He balked. It was a high price.

"What about seven bronze coins?" Aten asked.

"We are not here to barter," Roth cut in quickly, digging into his pocket. "We are here to respect the laws Arlo has in place."

He placed the silver coins in her hand. She nodded and turned around, not paying them any more attention as she walked to the card players.

"Two silver coins?" Aten said, "Is this a city of thieves?"

"It is not as if this is our money," Ren admonished him. Aten went quiet, nodding slowly. This was blood money. Money granted to him by the death of hundreds.

"Why do you think she wanted our names?" Aten asked.

"Perhaps they are in search of knights who are indebted to someone in Arlo?" Ren suggested.

Aten was dissatisfied with the answer but could not think of a better one. He looked up when he heard the melody of the lute come his way once more. He hurried toward the sound awkwardly, his leg not fully prepared for movement yet. Ren walked alongside him as he limped to quell the sensation of pain. He looked up, determined, and followed where the bard's song led him.

"If I do not collect you from the shops, we will meet back here in an hour," Ren said, looking over his shoulder. Parner waved them off as Trise and Gertrude tied the boat to the dock.

16

Aten's face whipped back and forth across the busy square, scoping out the noise. Among the merchants clamoring for attention, trying to undercut their competition of the children playing in the center, the lute played somewhere in the background. It felt like the strange song was shrouding the entire area, with no source. Hundreds of voices overlapped, the music tried to make itself heard over the sea of noise. Aten closed his eyes and listened intently.

"Do you not feel you are going a bit far?" Ren inquired.

"How do you mean?" Aten asked, tilting his head one way when he thought he located the origin once more.

"This is likely just another bard. You told us Pirulo was old and lived in the desert. Why would he venture so far North?" Ren asked.

"That is not the point, Ren. Yes, it was Pirulo who gave me the means to defeat Vesta, but he is a bard among many. Perhaps this bard will be just as wise!" Aten said.

"Yes, but even your search for bards is obsessive in that—"

"There!" Aten pointed across the square to a man playing his lute in front of a hat placed on the floor. It was not Pirulo, but just seeing a bard was enough to energize Aten.

He bolted away from Ren, limping as fast as he could to the musical artist. Once he arrived in front of him, Aten stood in awe, astounded to see another bard. He smiled and felt elated at the sight of the lute. It was an instrument of comfort to him after he had met Pirulo.

Around him the townspeople kept a wide berth, close enough to hear the music, but far enough to be spoken to by the bard without him raising his voice. Aten saw one man nudge another and gesture to Aten. They watched Aten smirking, as if they looked forward to the interaction he was about to have.

The lutenist was short and did not look to be much older than Aten. Aten's smile wavered when he heard the bard play. It was not very reminiscent of Pirulo's music. It was much more cacophonous and staccato than the melodious rhythms Pirulo put together to make his speech sound like a ballad. More than a few incorrect notes were played in the few seconds Aten had been standing there. The hat in front of him had less than a handful of coins, all of them bronze. Ren walked next to him and looked to Aten with a raised eyebrow.

"He is terrible," Ren declared quietly.

"He is... not the best," Aten agreed.

The bard began to play faster, his face eager for the audience of two in front of him. He ran a scale up and down and then waited for a dramatic moment before he began speaking,

"Hello there, I'm Karn, how nice to meet you

I've never met you, are you just passing through?

If you have time, stay and listen for a while

I think you will enjoy your time"

Ren and Aten looked to one another.

"He cannot rhyme consistently?" Ren asked, stifling a laugh.

"He may still be knowledgeable in some things," Aten shrugged, his ambitions for this meeting dwindled by the moment.

Karn continued to play quickly, desperate to keep their attention.

"Karn we have come to ask you for your help with something. Are you familiar with dra—"

"Ah, so you have come for my sound advice!

Know that everything I share comes at a price!" Karn sang quickly, kicking the hat in front of him a few inches forward for effect. He strummed a few chords, many of them dissonant, and stood expectantly.

Aten rolled his eyes, then suddenly remembered something Vesta had told him,

If you happen to meet any bards, be sure to tip well, they are normally sticklers for information.

It made him uncomfortable that she had advised him well when he went in search of information to kill her. He tilted his head toward Ren who dug a hand into his pocket, jingling with coins. Karn's eyes gleamed at the sound, and he swallowed hard in anticipation. Ren tossed one bronze coin into the hat. Karn frowned, and played a few more notes, pointing to the hat once more with his foot. Ren scoffed and dropped a second bronze coin.

"What knowledge do you seek?

I would be happy to provide what you seek." Karn lowered his head in deference to the pair. Ren closed his eyes and looked away, stifling another laugh.

"What do you know of dragons, bard?" Aten asked, his enthusiasm lackluster.

Karn smiled like he had answered this question many times before, then began reciting,

"I know many things whether in future or historical,

I am no mere bard, no, I am an oracle
Knowledge of dragons, I know many tales
Incredibly strong, though they look frail
I studied their wars when I was in youth
In their hearts lies a weakness, that is truth"
Ren nodded, bored and turned to Aten.

"Well it seems he does not know much more than—"

His voice caught when he saw the scrutiny Aten was giving the young musician. Features were slowly hardening on his face as fire ignited in his eyes. The townspeople in the vicinity were snickering, satisfied at watching another pair of tourists be conned by Karn.

"You are... an oracle?" Aten asked sharply.

"That I am, the future I hold,
whether you die young or will grow old," Karn sang.

"Have you—" Aten breathed steeply, he was trembling ever so slightly.

"What ails you?" Ren asked, worried.

"Have you ever discussed dragons with others?" Aten asked, his teeth firmly grit together.

Karn's eyes went up playfully and he nodded to his hat once more.

"We are done here," Ren scowled at Karn, putting his arm around Aten to pull him away. Aten remained rigid.

"Pay him," Aten commanded.

"What? He has not even earned his first payment, let us leave the fool," Ren said indignantly.

Aten shoved a hand down Ren's pocket and pulled out a coin. It was silver. Ren gasped.

"Roth, do not pay him that much, it is more than he deserves to earn in a year's time with his lack of talent," Ren said sternly.

Aten and Karn were looking squarely at one another, ignoring all of Ren's utterances. Karn licked his lips slowly.

"I pay this and you answer all of my questions?" Aten asked slowly.

Karn nodded his head quickly, his fingers caressing his lute desperately.

Aten tossed the coin in the hat. Ren groaned and rubbed his temples. The onlookers went into complete hysterics at this point. One of them pointed while trying to contain his howling laughter,

"The jester finally found someone at his level! A boy moronic enough to pay him for making a mockery of our town!"

Ren went flush, but Aten paid him no mind, his steely gaze locked onto Karn.

"Have you ever discussed dragons with others?" Aten repeated.

"Yes, I have, it was—"

Karn suddenly realized he was neither singing nor playing. He strummed an untuned chord and continued melodically,

"Yes I have, it was a group of six from the Kolog capital

They told me they came through the Pleasant Plains"

"Who were they?" Aten asked, his hands tightening into fists. Ren stared with a mix of fascination and horror at the state of Aten.

"I know not of their names or where they were from at all

But one held a hammer, one a bow, and the others I do not recall

They asked about a dragon to the Southwest

I told them strike its heart and then they went Southwest

I knew a knight would be nearby

For Pallas would always send one to die"

Karn began inching toward his hat, peering into the small pile of coins. Aten was shaking. He marched forward while Karn dove toward his money quickly in a panic, squatting like a chicken over eggs.

"Sorry, all payments are nonrefundabl—"

"Aten!" Ren called in shock.

Karn was flat on his back, his eyes glass balls floating around their sockets and drifting in different directions. The area below his eye was swelling quickly and he groaned slowly, placing a hand on his head and blinking.

"He answers your questions and you strike him?" Ren asked, pulling Aten aside aggressively.

"This bard killed the Royal Guard of the North! He fed the madman Tholen a false prophecy and sent him on a crusade to kill me! He is the reason I cannot raise my left arm over my head today! He is the reason Roth is dead! He—He—" Aten looked at the young bard, still regaining his senses, "He has to face consequences of his actions."

As Aten's labored breath slowly subsided, he realized the noise surrounding him had gone quiet. The townspeople were watching him. He looked to the ground, uncomfortable with the attention only to be met with Karn's wobbly gaze as he was picking his head off the brick floor.

"Did you hit me?" he asked, dumbfounded.

Aten tried to find a happy medium between looking apologetic and glaring at the person who single handedly lied enough to leave Kolog all but defenseless.

"He paid you to do it," Ren jumped in, brandishing a bronze coin and tossing it into the hat. Karn laid his head back on the ground dumbly.

"Very well," he said, satisfied. He reached for his lute to play more dissonant chords while his eye slowly turned the color purple.

Ren placed an arm around Aten and led him away from the town square smiling at the onlookers and looking for Parner and the others. Aten kept his eyes on his feet, listening to the gossip being exchanged around him as he was escorted away from the witnesses to his attack.

"—you see what the knight did?"

"—an impressive punch, even King Apoph—"

"—hear what name he was called by the other knight—"

"—but poor Karn will have a black—"

Ren stopped him when they were comfortably out of earshot of more jeers or comments about the altercation. Aten was rubbing one hand with the other, pressing away the stinging sensation of having dealt the blow to Karn.

"That was the same oracle who spoke to Tholen and his party, then?" Ren asked.

"It has to be," Aten nodded.

"And are you satisfied with how you dealt with him?" Ren asked.

"I… I am," Aten admitted sheepishly.

"Excellent, let us be moving on. We need to find Parner and the others," Ren said, looking past Aten and walking along.

"You are not angry with me?" Aten asked, walking along with him.

"For hitting a conman who has certainly led countless others to their deaths in order to maintain his claim of being an oracle?" Ren asked, "I was surprised, yes, but I understand your sentiments. Especially given your state." Ren pointed to his shoulder.

"You have my thanks, Boros," Aten said.

"You must never act that way again, Roth. We are guests in this land and I do not wish to bring unnecessary conflict to either us or them. We want others allied with us when we ask them for assistance to kill a dragon," he looked in one direction, went pale and then briskly went in another direction.

N. T. Lazer

"Is Karn following us?" Aten asked not having been able to follow his gaze as he caught up.

"No, but the woman from the port is looking for someone," Ren said.

"Did she see us?" Aten asked.

"I do not know. Look! There is Parner at an armory!" Ren said, increasing his speed even more, causing Aten to have to readopt his limp to keep up.

"The bard was dissatisfactory, I take it?" Parner asked, turning to smile at them.

"In more ways than I could have considered," Aten nodded. "Did you find any food?"

"We are on the wrong end of town for food, so I purchased us some swords and Trise and Gertrude are next door purchasing arrows," Parner said, holding up three sheathes with swords.

"You left them alone?" Aten asked, upset.

"What would they do on their own that worries you?" Parner asked.

"I do not trust them. In fact, I think we should leave without them," Aten said simply.

"What a surprising answer," Parner said sarcastically, then lowered his voice, "I have spent my time alone here gathering information. Did you hear of the new King of Kolog?"

"New king?" Aten said, stunned.

"Without the Royal Guard of the North, they were weak and likely taken over by whoever coveted the power of the crown," Ren said.

Aten frowned and thought of Captain Brun, one of the last men alive after the massacre of the Royal Guard of the North. Another consequence of his acting too slowly. The entire course of the kingdom had changed at his delay. He shuddered.

"That is not the most imperative piece of information gathered here," Parner said conspiratorially, "the new king's name is A—"

"Boros!" a woman called from behind them. Ren went stiff while Parner looked up sharply, hoping he was not heard. The woman from the docks marched up to the three of them, fuming.

"I seem to very distinctly remember you promising me that you will keep this one out of trouble, hmm?" she asked, lowering herself to yell in Ren's face turning her head slowly to glare at Aten.

"Y-yes, but—"

"And did I just hear correctly that he wasted no time in charging in this town and attacking the oracle who plays in our square, leaving him purple in the eye and out of his wits?" she asked.

"You did what?" Parner asked, impressed.

"There are no such things as oracles," Aten offered, repeating what Vesta had taught him.

The woman wheeled around to look at him with her ferocious gaze, her nostrils flaring rapidly.

"You think I do not know that, you imbecile?" the woman spat.

Aten blinked, perturbed by the answer.

"You know this and you allow him to continue his practice?" he asked.

"Our richest repeat customers come to hear his wisdom and songs. And now they will see him with a welt on his face and wonder how he did not see that attack coming if he is truly an oracle! We will lose visitors and so we will lose customers. I cannot have the ruffian who did this in my town. You will need to leave," she said, standing at full height and pointing to the river.

Trise and Gertrude emerged from the building next door, their quivers fully stocked.

"What is happening?" Gertude asked, looking nervously between the knights and the woman.

"We are being asked to leave," Ren said, making his way back.

Trise scoffed.

"You expect us to just leave after what we paid you to enter—"

"I should be more clear," Ren cut in. "We are being asked to leave with good reason. We must be going."

Trise scoffed again, but said nothing more as she walked a few steps. She tripped, caught herself on the woman and continued, walking ahead of the group with a hand in her quiver. The group followed, all of them tailed by the imposing woman from the dock, making sure they made no delays in leaving Arlo. Aten's stomach growled loudly.

"Can we at least purchase some food, please? We have money," Gertude asked.

The woman thought for a moment, then shook her head.

"Leave in peace or leave in pieces," she offered.

The dock was soon right ahead of them. Aten sighed and went on board the boat, lamenting the fact he paid a small fortune of silver for no more than half an hour's time in the city of Arlo. Perhaps it was a city of thieves after all.

As soon as the boat was untied, the woman kicked the vessel from the dock and waved them off. Trise and Gertrude wasted no time in rowing away from the city. The woman was soon approached by a guard who told her something urgently. She looked up in shock and looked back at the boat, her face a mix of rage and confusion.

"Wait! Come back!" she commanded.

Trise scoffed and signaled to Gertrude to continue rowing away from the city.

"Why the sudden change of heart?" Parner asked his fellow passengers, passing the swords and sheaths he purchased to Aten and Ren.

"She may have realized I took this," Trise said, tucking her hand into her quiver and holding up the parchment the woman on the dock was holding earlier.

"Ha!" Parner laughed, excitedly, "what does it say?"

"I do not know," she said, wadding it up and tossing the parchment to Parner.

"You cannot read?" Parner asked, unwrinkling it.

Gertrude and Trise shook their heads.

"That is a…"

Parner looked at the parchment with consternation, shaking his head with disbelief.

"What is it, Parner?" Aten asked.

"It… It looks to be notes that the woman took. Just random words in a list," Parner said nonchalantly, signaling with his eyes that Aten should come next to him to read it.

Aten moved next to him and read down the list, his eyes growing with horror at every line:

- *New King of Kolog*
- *King Apophis*
- *Pallas*
- *Knight*
- *Aten*

17

"What is written, Parner?" Trise asked over her shoulder, her focus on rowing the boat.

"It... ummm..." he looked to Aten who shook his head rapidly. Parner waved the parchment emphatically, trying to silently relay the importance of revealing the information. Aten shook his head more rigorously, then pointed to one term on the page:

King Apophis.

"It seems there is a new King of Kolog, by the name of King Apophis," Parner said.

Gertrude dropped her oar and Trise stopped rowing altogether, turning around to scrutinize Parner.

"A-Apophis?" Gertrude said, her voice trembling as she fished her oar out of the water. "That is the name that the dying man in Berdun was trying to say, I am sure of it."

"We cannot be certain of that," Trise reminded.

"I am certain of it," Gertrude repeated, finally grabbing the oar and turning to look at the others on the boat.

"Does the writing mention anything else?" Trise asked.

Parner opened his mouth, then closed it to look at Aten from the corner of his eye. Aten wanted to shake his head once more, but not in front of the girls. Parner sighed, and spoke,

"The only other thing mentioned here is Pallas," Parner said begrudgingly.

"Pallas?" Trise and Gertrude said simultaneously.

"She made note of your hometown? The one that has been destroyed?" Trise asked.

Parner went quiet. Aten also looked away, ashamed of the reminder that he could do nothing to save his home, then nodded slightly.

"I apologize, I know the wound is still fresh," Trise said sincerely. "I owed that town a great deal."

"You did?" Gertrude asked, surprised.

"My father and so many others from Banti died in trying to slay the dragon that lived near there. I was told it would be fruitless to try and exact revenge upon Vesta. I was determined to try regardless, even if my life was to be forfeit. A foolish plan in hindsight. But now I have learned that a knight of Pallas killed the beast. The town has my thanks for the actions of this knight. While I regret not being able to take revenge myself, the best way I can think of to repay them is to follow Roth in his quest to slay a new dragon wreaking havoc on this land," Trise said, looking to Aten.

Aten's face went warm, but he frowned.

"I do not want your thanks," Aten spat.

"I told you! He has done it again!" Gertrude said to Trise.

"It is fine," Trise assured.

"Done what?" Ren asked, curious.

"Roth does not want anything to do with us. It was clear from the beginning that he does not wish to have us in his company, and even now he does not wish to speak to us!" Gertrude said.

Aten shrugged. The boat bumped into shore and continued drifting aimlessly. Ren picked up an oar and began rowing while the conversation continued.

"Why is it you distrust them?" Parner asked.

"I do not trust slavers. Is that so hard to understand?" Aten asked.

"No," Trise nodded, sympathetically. Gertrude looked at her like she expected her to say something different.

"Yes!" Parner said mischievously. "For if your story was true, then you did not treat even Vesta as harshly as you treat these two."

"You what!?" Gertrude yelled.

"That was different," Aten protested.

"You find us more threatening than a dragon?" Trise asked, amused.

"No, that is not... I do not wish to speak of it," Aten said, looking out to the river.

"Ah, but I do," Parner said happily, "And I will continue to speak of it until I am satisfied with your answer. You do not have to trust them, but I wish to know why."

"It is nothing, I simply do not like the archers who enslaved others," Aten said forcefully.

Gertrude looked to Trise again who shook her head.

"I am still not satisfied. Is it that you find yourself incomparable to them in terms of skill? Trise was able to hit this fish out of the air, do you envy that?" Parner asked, pointing to the remains of the skinned and gutted fish that Ren had left.

"No, it is nothing," Aten said firmly, his voice rising.

"Then maybe you find them a burden on you because now we have more mouths to feed?" Parner said, raising an eyebrow to Trise. Trise rolled her eyes.

"No!" Aten yelled.

"They are archers," Ren said thoughtfully.

Aten's heart went tight.

"Very perceptive of you," Parner mocked Ren, shaking his head smugly.

"Think of who caused him the worst damage after Vesta. Perhaps more damage than Vesta," Ren explained, rowing slowly while he deliberated.

Parner's eyes raced the floor of the boat in thought. He blinked and looked up.

"That madman, Tholen. The archer!" Parner exclaimed as the epiphany hit him.

Aten squirmed in his seat.

"Do you hate archers?" Parner asked energetically.

"I—I do not wish to speak of it…" Aten murmured, embarrassed.

"By God, it is true! You are too easy to read!" Parner pointed at him.

He roared out a boisterous laugh, then snatched Gertrude's bow from her and stood grandly on the boat, holding the bow high.

"I renounce my knighthood! I am an archer! How do you feel about me now?" Parner called to Aten.

"Stop Parner, it is not funny," Aten grumbled.

Trise scoffed, satisfied with the answer, and got up to assist Ren in rowing the boat. Gertrude sat with her eyes bulging, staring at Aten.

"You hate us for our ability to use a bow? How absurd can you be, Roth?" she asked. "I thought it reasonable that you hated what we were forced to become, but this…" she pointed to Parner who had taken on a waltz with Gertrude's bow, "this is foolish and ridiculous."

"I told you I did not wish to talk about it," Aten said.

"And I am glad we did so that I now know just how petty of a man you are," Gertude ridiculed.

Aten's eyes were locked with the floor, his breathing deep and forceful. He touched his wounded shoulder tenderly, then screwed his eyes shut when it still smarted with pain. A tear threatened to break through his eyes.

"I do not know if I will ever have use of my arm again. Not like I used to. I trusted that archer. He brought an army to kill me. He led to the death of R-Ro-my closest friend. He made me one of his party, then turned to stab me in the back," Aten said, his voice trembling.

"In the shoulder!" Parner corrected, pointing to the wound. Aten glared at him.

Gertrude's expression softened when she saw the moisture building in his eyes.

"That sounds difficult," she said, her voice gentle.

"Do you remember one of the first things Trise noticed of me when we were captured? Nothing of my countenance or even my knighthood. She mentioned my wounds. I do not wish to be identified by scars of my past mistakes," Aten said, upset.

Gertrude nodded compassionately.

"I understand. You are a Dragonslayer, Roth. You should be recognized by your accomplishments, not your betrayals. But I wish you would understand that we are nothing like that archer you met before. Trise is strong headed, but she is also very considerate and a pragmatic woman. And I would never do such a thing to an ally."

Parner stopped his mockery and sat down beside Aten, placing an arm on his good shoulder firmly.

"I would never let someone join us if they had the capacity to harm you, my brother," he said. "Even if they are dirty slavers."

Like before, Gertrude looked to Trise at the mention of slaves.

"If you do not tell them, I will," Gertrude warned.

Trise sighed.

"Very well. The women of Banti are no longer capturing or enslaving people. One of my last orders to them was to stop all such action," Trise admitted with a satisfied nod from Gertude to corroborate the claim.

"What? When?" Aten asked.

"After we gained more than enough money from Berdun to never again need such a form of finance," Trise answered.

"Why did you not tell us until now?" Ren asked.

"I did not care to. We did what we felt was necessary for our survival. Why should we not be judged for what actions we took? Roth slayed a dragon and we abducted travelers in order to accumulate wealth. Why should he not see us as he does? We are on different levels," Trise answered.

"We were not always like this!" Gertrude intruded, "We tried to live off of the land surrounding us, hunting in the woods to the south of Banti and gathering water from the river near us. But we were soon raided by bandits. Terrible, terrible bandits who took our money and some of our women. In turn, we became bandits ourselves to spread a reputation of fear in the area surrounding us. It worked in that we were safe, but it also came at the cost of our morals."

Aten looked to Gertrude, then to Trise, seeing them as wholly different people now. He blinked away the accumulating moisture in his eyes and felt for once that they were his allies. And powerful ones at that. He should not be wary of them, but look for ways that they can further his aim for defeating this new dragon. He breathed deeply, digesting all of these new feelings. Then he looked to them both with sincerity.

"My name is not Roth. It is Aten," he said to their surprise. Parner beamed at the revelation, happy to finally be past it.

Aten went on to explain everything he knew about dragons and what exactly the archers were getting themselves into.

18

The five travelers lay on the banks of the water, lit only by a small fire, eating the fraction of the fish each of them were given as dinner. They had reached the point where the river opened to the bank of Rowa Lake after following the south edge of the lake to Dervin. Aten stared at the stick he held, now sans fish. It was a very unsatisfactory meal, but Aten realized he was more content when there was a need for food rather than a need for water. He could drown his stomach's pleas for food. The small mouthful of fish he had reminded him of the large meal he shared with Vesta. He sighed at the thought. It seemed he could not get her out of his head.

Everything led back to Vesta, one way or another.

"You are Aten and you are Ren? You made up the names of Boros and Roth?" Trise asked, still processing the explanation Aten had given them before stopping for the evening.

"Ren and Boros are—were other knights of our guild," Aten said.

"The others who died defending Pallas?" Trise asked.

Aten looked down uncomfortably.

"Roth was the one that died when he came to Aten's aid in Vesta's cave during her battle with the Royal Guard of the North," Gertrude corrected gently.

"Ah, I remember. A good man, God rest his soul," Trise said with fervor.

He remembered how he felt at Roth's death. The utter powerlessness. The pain. He was writhing on the ground while his friend healed his wounds and was thrown aside so ruthlessly. He felt the small feeling of vindication for having killed Vesta when she did something so awful, but he also felt that powerlessness again. It seemed all of his actions since he met dragons were dependent on others. Ren and Parner carrying him out of Pallas and now Trise and Gertrude navigating their way to the Deserted Desert. He scowled to himself. A frustration was building within him.

"Can we fish for more?" Parner asked, clutching his stomach lightly.

"We may, but the window has passed," Ren said.

"The window?"

"Fish are hungriest at sunrise and sunset. It is well past sunset," Ren explained.

"Ah, well, perhaps there is a fish out there with a more unconventional appetite?" Parner asked.

"Like your own?" Ren asked.

Gertrude and Aten laughed while Trise smirked.

They stared into the fire for a few content moments before Aten shifted uncomfortably.

"Why do you suppose the King of Kolog and I show up on the same parchment from Berdun?" Aten asked.

"Suppose he has heard of your Dragonslaying and wants you to kill the new one? It is likely the beast has made itself known all over the kingdom, if not the world in its rage," Trise offered.

"That is a good theory," Parner agreed quickly, pointing to her. Ren smiled at him while he thought.

"I find it more likely that Apophis is looking to solidify his claim to the throne," Ren surmised. "A new king is likely wary of his subjects' loyalty, and what better way to do that than to show that a Dragonslayer endorses him?"

"He wishes to use me as a political pawn?" Aten asked.

"The capital city is under a new ruler who likely seized power by force when it was revealed how few of the Royal Guard of the North returned. The city will not take lightly of that fact," Trise nodded, coming around to the idea.

"Yes, I agree," Parner nodded to Trise. "A very good analysis."

"No, that does not make any sense," Aten shook his head. "How would anyone know I killed Vesta?"

"Merchants, Aten, merchants," Parner said. "They spread their wares and their tales equally. If the people of Pallas reached Kit, then the merchants of Kit went to Kolog, then we can be certain that Apophis heard of your feat. And the same way the news traveled to him, the news of his claim to the throne reached Arlo before we got there."

"Far too fast," Aten said uncertainly.

"Do not underestimate merchants," Gertrude said. "Why, it was only a week ago in Banti that a merchant passed through and let us know that a knight had fallen in love with the dragon in Vesta Forest. We took it for hearsay."

Aten briefly saw Vesta's face flash before him as she lay dying in her lair.

"Do you truly believe it defeatable?" Trise asked. "The new dragon? It seems that your defeat of Vesta was by luck."

"Of course! Her father will have a weakness just as she did!" Aten said emphatically.

"And you believe Pirulo will have knowledge of this secret weakness?" Trise asked.

"I do," Aten nodded.

Trise looked confused and looked as though she wanted to follow up, but Ren asked before she had the chance,

"When you asked Pirulo about how to defeat Vesta, did you ask about her by name?"

Aten thought back to it.

"I am uncertain. What difference does that answer make?" he asked.

"Aten…" Ren said slowly, hoping for him to come to the conclusion on his own, "if you asked Pirulo about how to defeat a nonspecific dragon, then why would his answer be any different this time than it was before?"

Aten's heart dropped. The frustration within him festered further.

"No, that is right, I did ask about Vesta," Aten said, not looking any of the four in the eyes.

"Are you certain?" Ren pressed. "It seems to me that we could save a lot of time and spend it making a surefire plan to strike its heart if we no longer need to revisit the Deserted Desert."

"What does it matter?" Aten yelled, upset. "If Pirulo had enough wisdom to dispense to help me kill Vesta, then we can be certain that he will be invaluable in our plans to kill this new dragon! We must go to see him!"

"Why are you so keen to go back to this bard?" Parner asked.

"He is wise! And he helped me when I was at the brink of death in the desert. I expect that he can help me again, now, when I have returned to that feeling of being on the brink of death, wondering if the dragon lies behind any given corner," Aten said.

In truth, Aten was clinging to that which gave him a semblance of control over his life. He had been carried along for so many steps of this journey by others, and he wanted to contribute something to this battle. He knew Pirulo would have something valuable to grant them, whether it was directly related to the new dragon or not. And he wanted to be the one to encourage them to get that wisdom to lead them to victory.

"I will follow you regardless, Dragonslayer," Trise said. Aten nodded to her gratefully, though he was still uncomfortable by how willing she was to help when she only came to know the truth about him mere hours ago. He felt that she was a very genuine person behind her frowns and steely gazes. "For now," she continued, "it is best we prepare to go to Dervin tomorrow. It will be on our way and we still require food for the trip South."

"Very well," Ren nodded. "I will take the first watch."

"First watch?" Aten asked.

"You expect me to allow us to be caught as easily as we were by these two again? No, we will share in the responsibility of taking watches from now on," Ren declared.

The others nodded.

"And we shall spar," Parner said, scouring the lake's edge for sizable sticks.

"We shall?" Aten flexed his shoulder nervously.

"Aye," Parner tossed him a stick that Aten fumbled and dropped to the ground. "We used to train in the guild. It is gone now, so we shall spar one another to keep up our wits in battle."

"A good plan," Ren agreed, a small twitch downward at the edge of his lips.

"But… my arm is not yet—"

"No excuses Aten. Your enemies will not ask whether your arm is up for a battle, they will only try to deal you killing blows," Parner reminded him, picking up another stick and wielding it like a sword.

Aten thought back to when they tried to escape their containment in Banti and Trise was easily able to best him in combat. He hated to be so weak. He wished for more control over his life, and such training could help. He picked up the stick and held it in front of him defensively.

"Can we take off our armor?" Aten asked, tired of having worn in all day.

"Not unless you intend to fight the dragon without armor," Parner replied.

Aten seriously thought that over. It was not as if the armor made much of a difference against a dragon. But it was good to learn to fight against other humans as well. He sighed, resigning himself to wearing the armor a bit longer.

"To the death?" he joked. He noticed Parner took a glance at Trise and Gertrude to make sure they were watching. They sat up, looking as though seated in a theater, waiting for the show to begin. It seemed like Parner wanted one of them to be watching before his focus snapped back to Aten. Perhaps it was his imagination.

"To the death!" Parner charged forward and thrust at Aten's gut, leaving him barely enough time to parry and stumble backwards. Parner immediately moved in closer, swiping at Aten's bad leg and Aten had to make another clumsy move back to avoid it, but used the space between them to swing his weapon down to Parner's head. Parner lifted his stick and blocked the attack, but dropped it as soon as the two branches made contact.

Aten and Parner looked at the stick on the floor awkwardly. Parner's face went a shade pink.

"You dropped your sword," Aten pointed out.

"A stick feels a bit different than a hilt when stuck," Parner explained as he went to pick it up.

"Sounds like an excuse to me," Aten teased.

Parner smiled and drew his stick like a sword once more and immediately spun to attack Aten's bad shoulder. Aten dropped his stick when struck, crying out sharply as the pain exploded from his wound.

"That was dirty!" he yelled, upset.

"Was it? My sparring partner always went for my slow spots and never went easy when it came to my injuries. I feel our enemies would do the same," Parner replied, tossing his stick between his hands energetically.

"It was just an easy way for them to win bouts against you, not a cunning strategy," Aten complained, rubbing the wound.

"I do not believe so. Roth was my sparring partner," Parner said.

Aten remembered that to be true. As much as he hated the cheap attack, he knew it was a vulnerable target and he would have to learn to fight others with the disadvantage. He felt both relieved and upset that Parner was not holding back on him. Parner pointed with his stick and spoke,

"You dropped your—"

"Shut up Parner," Aten picked up his weapon and prepared for another series of blows.

The two sparred for almost a hundred bouts, many of which Parner was able to win by exploiting Aten's weak points. But as the battles progressed, Aten was able to prepare for the swings that were intended for his wounds and maneuver himself out of the way, finding weak points in Parner's form. When Parner attempted to strike Aten's shoulder, he left his bicep open to be stabbed lightly. Enough to leave a terrible wound if hit with a blade. And when he tried to strike Aten's leg, his neck was always stuck out too far. Aten did not know whether he was getting better at reading Parner's movements or simply getting better at reading any potential opponent, but he was too tired to try and figure that out.

The further they went in fighting, the more desperate their swings and the more damage they took at their openings.

"You rely too much on your anger, Aten," Ren said from the fire. "You will exhaust yourself of anger before you exhaust yourself of your wits. Try to exercise patience, parrying easy blows until they slip up."

"Right," Aten breathed, sweat dripping from both him and Parner.

He tried to be more patient, but he was simply too tired to continue blocking everything Parner had to throw his way. It only made him more frustrated, which made him lash out, which earned him more injuries, which made him more frustrated. It was a very painful cycle.

By the end of it, both Aten and Parner were covered in welts, particularly over their arms and necks. Aten's shoulder and leg burned furiously and he looked forward to being able to sleep off the pain. He and Parner stumbled back to the campfire and collapsed, shedding off their armors to sleep in their tunics. He and Parner stared up at the stars, heaving in exhaustion.

"Was it wise to attack Aten's wounds? You could have reopened them," Gertrude pointed out.

"A fantastic observation that would have been far more appreciated before we began sparring," Parner said in between deep breaths.

"I am fine... I think," Aten said, checking his bandages to see if anything looked out of the ordinary. His legs were bruised and purple all over, but nothing seemed like it required immediate attention.

"You fight well," Trise said to them both. Parner beamed.

"But I am far better, yes? Poor Aten was like an old man compared to my speed and ferocity," Parner said.

"In truth, I believe Aten could have easily bested you if it was not for his injuries," Trise answered.

"Ha! Even an old man could beat you," Aten said, his eyes closed.

"You could barely keep up!" Parner said, "It was as... between your..."

Aten drifted off to sleep.

Aten entered Vesta's lair. She was examining her claws, a hole in her heart. She looked up at him expectantly.

"I told you I would destroy villages if you were to leave me alone," Vesta said, looking at him disappointed.

"This is not your work, but the work of your father," Aten answered. He was holding the hilt of the dagger he had used to kill her.

"You should return to me," she said.

"You… you are dead," Aten told her.

Vesta did not answer, only retracted her claws and stared at him.

"Do you know how to kill your father?" Aten asked.

"If you wish to kill my father, you will return to me," Vesta answered.

Aten shuddered nervously. He understood that she was telling him he would die if he were to face her father.

Vesta suddenly burst into flames and in the flash of light was replaced by her father. He laughed and flashed forward with one flap of his wings, breathing white-hot flame into his face. Aten opened his eyes in shock only to be similarly blinded by the rising of the sun on the horizon. He wondered when the nightmare would end.

19

Aten rubbed his eyes and looked at the sun reflecting off the water, surprised to see Parner awake and Ren asleep off to the side. He stifled a yawn and went to sit next to his fellow awoken knight, who he found had set up various fishing poles fashioned from sticks from the bank similar to the ones they fought with the night before.

"You did not wake me for my watch," Aten greeted him.

"You did not wake," Parner answered quietly, his eyes watching the water. "And Ren told us fish would be hungry at sunrise. I wished to catch breakfast."

"Ah," Aten nodded, watching the water flow gently past them. "Any luck?"

"If by 'luck' you mean marvelous skill, then yes," he pointed to a circle of rocks that was surrounding a small but impressive pile of fish. There was a fish for each of the travelers.

"All of them together would hardly make an appetizer for you," Aten joked.

Parner smirked, his eyes still unfocused on something in the distance.

"You are awfully quiet. Are you well?" Aten asked.

"Our home is gone," Parner rubbed a bruise in his bicep.

"Well... Yes, that it is. We knew this?" Aten said uncertainly.

"I have just come to realize that this dragon has given us nowhere to return. No place to call home after this quest."

"We will have Kit to regroup with the others of Pallas," Aten replied.

"That is not our home, it is a place to take shelter while a dragon ravages the land," Parner said, blinking abruptly. "We fled. I fled, Aten. I did not even fight for my village."

"You said it yourself, Parner. We would have collectively died had you not helped me out of there," Aten protested.

"Hmm..." Parner mused, blinking again. Aten noticed his eyes were glistening. Again, he felt strange that his comrades were able to experience such emotions when thinking of loss of life and his home, but he was left with nothing but frustration within him.

Aten stared at his brother in arms a minute longer before realizing Parner did not wish to speak of it anymore. Parner wiped his eyes and looked out to the water, lost in thought again. They sat at the water's edge in silence until Ren roused himself and rolled to an upright position.

"Anything to report?" he asked the two knights. Gertrude and Trise stirred, getting up one after another.

"There were a few boats that passed us in the night, all of them from Arlo to Dervin. And I caught us something to break our fasts," Parner gestured to the fish.

"Multiple boats passed us overnight? Why would they travel the water at night?" Trise asked as she went to the lake to splash water on her face.

"I do not know, but from the outlines of them in the darkness, I could see they were all armed," Parner replied.

"Strange… Why could they not wait until morning to travel?" Trise repeated the question, looking out to the ripples she caused.

"Perhaps they were raiders?" Gertrude suggested.

"Headed to Dervin?" Ren asked.

The group looked at one another all at once.

"Perhaps we should leave immediately?" Gertrude suggested. "So that we may assist Dervin if they have any trouble coming their way."

"The boats were too spread apart to be part of the same raid… I think," Parner said. "We should eat, then go."

"I agree. If anything, we would bring more trouble by taking him into town," Trise said pointing to Aten.

"Me? I am suddenly a menace to towns?" he snapped.

"Let me think. You have a dragon who seeks to kill you and burns down towns indiscriminately; your name shows up on a parchment in the city of Arlo, and you strike the first man you meet as soon as you set foot in a public square. None of these qualities are anything to worry about though, yes?" Trise asked.

Parner laughed as Aten stammered, unable to reply with anything substantial.

"Very well, breakfast then we set off," Ren said, squatting down to start a quick fire to cook the fish.

"I really think we should at least go to Dervin before eating. We can drink water to quench our hunger," Gertrude insisted.

"Water quenches thirst, not hunger!" Parner replied. "I require a meal!"

"Perhaps we should go to Dervin?" Aten offered. He did not have much of an opinion on potential raiders, but he did not wish to delay their trip to Pirulo if he had the means to do otherwise.

"Very well, let us be off," Trise said immediately.

"What? I thought you said he was a menace," Parner pointed at Aten.

"Yes, but if the Dragonslayer menace wishes to go then we shall go," Trise replied simply.

Aten stared at her dumbfounded. He turned to Ren who shrugged, just as surprised as he was.

"You would... follow my orders?" Aten asked.

"You avenged my father's death. I told you I would join you on this journey, not control it. I feel it is expected," Trise said. Gertrude nodded excitedly, tossing her bow into the boat and hopping inside.

Aten stared at Gertrude, followed by Trise, then Ren, and lastly the flabbergasted Parner who was looking at his fish longingly before begrudgingly grabbing them to take aboard.

"Let us be off, then!" Aten said, gathering his sword, armor, and practice stick while joining Gertrude on the boat.

The boat ride was quaint and mostly uneventful. Aten tried his hand at some fishing, watching his rod intently for anything that would take the bait on his line. Parner's appetite for speaking increased as his appetite for breakfast grew more voracious. Ren offered to row the boat today, but was rejected by Gertrude and Trise who decided that since neither of them had taken watch or caught fish, they were obligated to row the way to Dervin. Given no other option to pass the time, Ren kept a close eye on the water, likely trying to find the boats that passed the night before.

Aten felt a tug at his rod and pulled it as hard as he could, revealing a line devoid of bait. He sputtered, disappointed. He could not even provide simple food for his group of followers. All he had was the wisdom of Pirulo to offer. He felt the ball of frustration within him grow further.

"So soon?" Ren said, gesturing to something on the horizon.

Aten followed his gaze to find a city at the edge. It looked to be at the intersection of the lake and another river headed south, bustling with activity. Dozens of boats filled its ports and people moved on and off boats in succession.

"By God, I have never seen so many people," Parner said in awe.

The port alone was as populated as the town square of Arlo with hundreds of voices beginning to make their way to the boat from Dervin's own square. Aten surmised that the amount of people in the city could have eaten the entirety of Pallas's crops in a single day. They looked to be people of all ages, men, women, and children traveling the city together. Aten had previously thought this would be the size of the Capital Cities of Kolog or Torn, but now had to reevaluate his definition of a large city.

Watch towers were dispersed along the edges of the city in more than just its cardinal directions. Each tower was equipped with its own pile of branches, used as a form of signal to other cities on the border of Rowa Lake. Aten could see each of them had two men within them watching the horizons of the city. He wondered if they had heard of the dragon.

"Dervin is a trade town. It has good relations with Ro, Stanus, and Arlo, so most people meet here to do business," Trise told the boat.

"Ro and Stanus? I thought they were part of the Kingdom of Torn," Parner asked.

"They are," Gertrude nodded, "but Torn knows its citizens get more benefit with access to Dervin than without, so they turn a blind eye even when they play as if they are prepared to declare war at the slightest challenge to their sovereignty."

"Does it look as though there are more boats than usual? As though they have been visited by raiders?" Parner asked.

"Difficult to tell," Gertrude admitted. Trise shrugged.

"Sounds to me as though we have nothing to worry about," Parner said, stretching confidently.

"That is not what I said," Gertrude said.

"I would prefer to avoid any unnecessary conflict," Ren added.

"Unless you believe there to be immediate danger, I would prefer we dock to gather the needed supplies. Unless you have other ideas you think would fare better," Aten decided.

"Very well…" Gertrude said quietly. "We will dock."

Aten steeled himself, stowing the fishing rod and preparing his sword in case the city was overrun by bandits. But by the looks of it, the town was bustling with activity and excitable merchants. And merchants meant the spread of information. Aten was almost certain they would have heard of the dragon.

"Let us hope the charge to stay in their port is a fraction of Arlo's," Ren said, patting his pocket of coins.

"And let us hope there are fewer bards for Aten to grant black eyes," Parner said.

Aten smiled sheepishly as Trise laughed alongside Parner.

As they pulled into the dock, a guard from a watchtower overlooking the water pointed at the boat in earnest.

"Knights! Knights!" he screamed, ringing a bell manically.

The attention of a handful of armed guards locked in on the group of knights and archers. One of them, a leader presumably, signaled to members of his battalion on the sidelines of the port with bows and arrows, who drew immediately.

Aten and Parner readied their swords and Trise and Gertrude their bows. Ren ducked slightly behind the boat's edge, gripping tightly to his undrawn weapon.

"What business do knights have in our city?" the leader of the guards asked menacingly.

20

Aten breathed slowly, assessing the situation. He began counting the number of assailants in his head and kept himself sharp, though he was clumsy in the sway of the boat. Trise looked to him for a signal which he was on the brink of delivering, but feared that those around him would lose their lives in their retaliation. There were twelve guards total, five swordsmen, six archers, and the leader who stood before them unarmed, awaiting their response. The leader was a head taller than Aten, and had twice the muscle as the knight. He glared at the five of them with a ferocity that would make a small child cry.

"Please, this is a misunderstanding, we mean you no harm," Ren said, his arms up placatingly as he slowly rose from the boat.

"Save your breath, Ren. They drew on us without speaking first," Aten told him.

"I am Ren. This is Parner, Trise, Gertrude, and Roth! We are passing through to Sekoa and were hoping to purchase supplies on the way!" Ren continued undeterred.

The leader did not react to the information, but did not order his men to move on them either. Aten grew impatient at the lack of action and thought he might be able to dive at the leader and take him hostage to diffuse the situation. Ren spoke again,

"We come from Banti, we—"

"Lies!" the leader spat. "We know Banti has no men of age living among the women there. Especially not knights."

Aten frowned. This was a town filled with traveling merchants. They would not be deceived by any trick of the tongue. He crept closer to the edge of the boat, preparing to jump off.

"It is not a lie. The women with us are from Banti. In truth, we are from Pallas, the three of us knights," Ren said. Parner and Aten's eyes flitted to him with unease.

"The former inhabitants of Pallas reside in Kit now, with a few of them breaking off to try their hand in Stanus. Do not play me for a fool," the guard said, though his composure tightened when he heard the term 'Pallas.'

"Were the knights of the guild with them?" Ren asked.

The question hung in the air for a moment as the leader turned to glance at his men. A few of them shook their heads in response to Ren's question. The leader nodded and turned back.

"Why are the knights here and not among their people?" the leader asked menacingly.

Ren swallowed.

"Because we are cowards who fled the battle that killed our brethren," Ren said, his voice shaky.

The guard's eyes narrowed. Suddenly, the leader let out a guffaw and clapped his hands together in hysterics. He pointed and laughed at the passengers of the boat then howled in the air, louder than before. His men joined in chuckling, but none of them lowered their weapons or stances. Aten stood confused, the intensity driven out of him. He could not decide if this was the best or worst time to attempt to dive at the large man.

"You are knights and allowed not only for the destruction of your property, but the death of your comrades! Lower your weapons men, these boys have neither the courage nor the dignity to incur injury to any of you!" the leader said between laughter.

Aten opened his mouth to protest, but Ren placed a hand on his shoulder and gripped tightly. Aten looked to see him shaking his head lightly. They had to endure the humiliation. The subordinates to the large man began to laugh along with him, the entire dock turning their attention toward the small crew aboard the boat.

"Look at this one in front!" the leader pointed to Aten. "He stood with his blade drawn as though he was ready to act in a moment's notice! And he was! Ready to turn tail and dive into the water as soon as negotiation went sour! His bruises look as though they were dealt by branches while running through dense woods! And that one there was ready to wet his tunic the moment I stood before them!"

Ren's face went red.

"And this one! He looks the type to convince others to run fool's errands, eh? Dragged women from their work in Banti to get them to go to Sekoa with a promise of money that he does not have!" the leader continued, sticking a thumb at Parner.

"Ha!" Parner laughed along with the others. "That does sound like me, eh!"

Trise and Gertrude looked at the display of guards with disappointment.

"Surely you can do better than be among these men?" the leader asked the archers. "Stay with us in Dervin? I am sure you will be treated well by me and my men here."

Trise opened her mouth with disgust in her eyes but Gertude spoke before she got the chance,

"Perhaps on our way back! We are women of our word and promised to continue our journey with the knights to its end."

The leader nodded with respect.

"Very well, come out of your vessel so that we may examine you and its contents," he said to all of them, flicking his head to call over two guards.

"Examine us?" Aten asked, slowly moving to sheath his blade.

"Aye, no one gets into the city unless Captain Torbough gives you permission," one of the guards said as he approached the boat. "No illegal materials, no Kingdom of Torn currency, and no stowaways."

"Money from Torn? What is the problem with their money?" Parner said, getting out of the boat and pulling out his blade for a guard to look over.

"Why do you ask?" Captain Torbough asked, towering over Parner, "you have some of their wealth among you?"

"No," Parner said, emptying his pockets and revealing the pile of money in his pocket. To Aten's surprise neither the captain nor the guards gave so much as a raised eyebrow to the display of wealth. They did not have Arlo's greed.

"Quite a bit of money you have on you," Torbough said casually, watching as Gertrude pulled her pockets inside out for the second guard combing over her belongings. "Where did you get that?"

"We are from Banti," Trise said. "Where else would we get this money but Berdun?"

"Ah," Torbough smiled mischievously. "You were able to access Berdun's wealth?"

"That is right. We left Banti with more people than we came here with," Trise answered honestly.

"A lot more people by the looks of it," a guard said, looking at the collective money between the group of them.

"About half a dozen," Trise said, thinking back to it.

"I heard the girls of Banti were strong, but I did not expect you to be able to capture and sell so many at a time," Torbough chuckled to himself.

Aten watched the conversation closely. He was hardly able to keep up with Trise's answers. She spoke the truth, yet sounded like she was telling a different story entirely. He was fascinated and wished he could have such a control over language when speaking to hostile individuals.

"Here I was thinking it was one of you having robbed the young man in Arlo," the captain said, waving a hand over the three knights.

"Who told you we robbed someone?" Parner asked, replacing his sword in his sheath as the guard went around him to look inside the boat.

"I was told by a merchant last night that one of you had knocked the 'oracle' there flat on his back, leaving him a bruise darker than a plumb. I assumed you took his money and ran," the captain said.

"He hardly had any money to begin with," Aten protested.

"Ah, so you did hit him?" the captain said with a raised eyebrow. He turned to tower over Aten who looked back up at him daring him to insult him.

"Good on ya!" the captain hollered, smacking him on the back hard enough to make Aten stumble a few feet forward. "I hated that Karn ever since he told lies about Dervin here, marring our good name for a few extra coins."

The two guards went to the rest of the crew, searching for any spots to hide weapons and made sure that the blades they carried were free of any poisons. One guard hopped aboard the boat, picking up each of the fish that Parner had caught that morning. Aten went wide eyed as he realized that within their possessions was the parchment from Arlo, revealing the information about there being a connection between King Apophis and Knights of Pallas. And Aten.

"Nothing here but trash," the guard announced, waving the collection of fish to Torbough.

"It is called breakfast," Parner replied coolly.

Aten kept his eyes on the ground. He did not know which of them held the parchment, but he did not want to give away the information with his expression. He had learned he was bad at hiding information.

"All right, you look fine. Apophis will have no interest in you," the captain said, calling his two guards away from the five travelers with another flick of his head.

"Apophis? You know of the new king?" Ren asked.

Captain Torbough's face went sour in an instant and all the guards that heard the question shifted uncomfortably.

N. T. Lazer

"He searches for a knight. And so we search for the knight as well. A Dragonslayer named Aten, though we are not to refer to him as 'Dragonslayer Aten,' as it offends the king. We are to capture him alive and send him to the capital city of Kolog," one of the guards explained.

Aten's stomach turned to ice; he strained to keep his face from emoting.

"You search for the knight, 'Oton,' even though the king is still fresh to the throne? How did he win your loyalty so soon, especially with you being so capably independent on your own?" Parner asked.

Torbough's features softened at the compliment.

"You speak as if you are unfamiliar with the king's power. He offered us protection. Guaranteed it if we did his bidding," the captain said.

"You... do not look as though you require his protection," Ren said, gesturing to the guards at the port.

"After hearing about what happened to Pallas... And after seeing the smoke that came from what looked to be somewhere near Berdun... I am in no place to reject the offer. The life of one knight seems to pale in comparison to what is being done so long as he lives," the captain said begrudgingly.

Aten's heart dropped into his cold stomach. The king was offering protection from the dragon.

But there was a small comfort in knowing that they had come here before any merchants informed them of Berdun's destruction. They had information to use.

"The knight's… life?" Aten asked, looking up to the captain with what he hoped was with no expression.

"I do not know what Apophis wants with Dragonslay—With Aten the Knight, but I do not believe that Aten would be an ally," the captain said gravely.

Aten shuddered. It seemed everywhere he went he was met with enemies, even as far up as the King of Kolog. The only one who thought well of him to begin with was Vesta. He shook her out of his head for yet another time.

All things led back to Vesta.

With that, Parner went to gather the fish and the travelers made their way inside of the city. They only spent a fraction of the cost to leave their boat docked in Dervin compared to Arlo. His companions kept close to Aten, as if to obstruct others from being able to view him. Aten noticed how slowly they were walking when they collectively followed his speed. He was grateful for them. They followed his awkward gait up until they were far from the port.

"It seems as though—"

"No!" Parner stopped Ren. "We shall share theories over breakfast, lest my stomach speak over all of your thoughts!"

Aten could not help but smile as the others consented through nods and shrugs. Parner hurried to find himself an area within the massive city lacking foot traffic and Gertrude hurried off in the opposite direction. Aten pointed to a place against one of the walls next to the port and Parner bounded over, wiping away detritus and setting up a few rocks for a fire. Gertrude returned with a few rocks and twigs in her hands.

"Spark rocks and wood for a small fire. I saw someone selling them right up the—"

"God bless you, Gertrude," Parner said gratefully, snatching the items from her hand and running the rocks over one another to start the fire. By the time Aten had settled himself in a comfortable position that would bother neither his shoulder nor his leg, Parner was already cooking the first fish.

"You may present your theories," Parner nodded to Ren.

"It seems the king plans to use you as an example? Or perhaps to force you to work under him?" Ren said, his eyes looking up to the watchtower nearest to them in thought.

"Or perhaps to simply kill him?" Trise said.

"I believe that he wants to kill me, as well," Aten agreed.

"That does not make sense," Ren shook his head. "If he wanted you dead, then why ask to have you captured rather than killed by these cities? I feel there is something more to it. What could a new king gain from having a Dragonslayer dead?"

"He could want to place the blame of Pallas on Aten?" Parner offered, looking at the fish closely.

"Why—How would he… what?" Aten asked three questions at once.

"Anderson looked as though he wanted to do it, perhaps Apophis thinks the same way," Parner offered.

"Anderson was afraid of losing his position among the people," Aten countered.

"Apophis wants to protect his position as well. And who better to claim the throne than someone who can claim to protect the people of Kolog from the dragon threat? The Dragonslayer!" Parner said grandly. He offered the first fish to Trise and smiled when she took it and began to tear through it.

Aten thought about his claim. It did seem plausible. But again, why would the king not ask for him to be executed if that was the case? Aten could not think of anything satisfying as an answer. He hated being left so confused and vulnerable. Parner handed him a fish next.

The five ate one by one as Parner gave them each their morning's food. Aten looked around the town, impressed by the inside of it as much as he was the outside. A series of watchtowers covered the entire circumference of the city, each of them with a guard dedicated to watching the comings and goings of Dervin. The people were bustling, children with food and toys in hand and men at stalls encouraging every passerby to give their wares some attention. The buildings were all massive, the smallest of them the size of the Knight's Guild of Pallas, which could hold all of the knights who lived in the village. The people here looked well-fed, as though poverty were stricken from this area long ago. By looking at them, Aten understood what Captain Torbough had meant that his life paled in comparison to this sprawling city.

He felt so small.

Even Berdun, as vile as the city may have been, was likely teeming with its own life of people, each with their own stories and plans for their lives, only to be cut down by a monster Aten wrought upon them. Perhaps that was why the king wanted Aten dead. To pay for what he had done to the kingdom by killing Vesta.

All things led back to Vesta.

After the five of them finished eating, they split up to purchase supplies for the trip through the Deserted Desert to find Pirulo. Ren went on his own in search of a map of the kingdom. Trise and Gertrude went in search of waterskins that could withstand the harsh climate of the desert. Parner offered to join, but they suggested he get the food with Aten, to which he agreed—after all, Parner was afraid of eating unpleasant meals selected by anyone other than himself.

As soon as Parner found a place that sold food, he planted a small pile of gold and silver coins on the counter, much to the elation of the shopkeeper, and began pointing to each of the different cuisines that interested him. Given the sheer quantity of food Parner purchased, the shopkeeper even threw in an extra bag to hold all of the food.

The shopkeeper was a stout woman, with calloused hands as rough as rocks. She had bags hanging casually below her eyes, as though sleep was not something she was too familiar with, but was able to smile and make small talk with her customers nonetheless.

"What do you plan to do with all of this food? A feast?" she asked, stacking dried meats on one end of the bag as she made room for the potatoes.

"Many small feasts, I hope," Parner said his hands tapping the counter in excitement.

"You are traveling, then?" she asked, placing the sack of food in front of Aten to take. Evidently, she believed him to be Parner's vassal. Aten picked it up regardless.

"Yes! Going to the Deserted Desert to get away from it all. The new king, the dragon, the burning villages. Just hope to have some peace of mind, eh?" Parner answered animatedly. The woman

N. T. Lazer

looked at him quizzically for his answer, but shrugged and continued.

"I have not heard of dragons outside of the legends of their wars that used to ravage our lands. I really did think them only legends. I did not think them real until one came to attack a town in the Kolog Kingdom," she said rather frightfully.

"Did you not hear of the dragon that resided in the forest West of Pallas?" Aten asked.

"I thought it was a folktale shared there to keep the children away from the forest. It could have been anything in the forest. I had no reason to believe it a dragon," she shrugged.

Aten stared, both amazed and offended that she believed his hometown's trials which had lasted years were no more than legend. He did not know how to respond reflecting that idea. Parner saw the look in his eyes and spoke quickly,

"Well, we best be off!"

"Have a safe voyage!" she called behind them.

"The ignorance in this town is worse than the greed in the last," Aten said to Parner as they left.

"Oh come on," Parner shook his head. "Why be so quick to draw hostility? She is a simple woman and leads a simple life. She does not want to live in a world with such a destructive creature."

Aten took his words to heart. He *was* quick to see her negatively, despite her only being misinformed on something that did not affect her. He wondered why he went to insult her so soon. He did not speak to her for more than a few seconds.

Within an hour, Aten, Parner, Trise, Gertrude, and Ren were all back at the dock, stocking their supplies for the long travels ahead. Ren was proud to present his map and point out their whereabouts. Trise and Gertrude had two waterskins for each of them, each made of leather. Aten looked at his new belongings on the boat and realized he had never once been this wealthy before. It was an odd sensation, and one he was not pleased to experience on top of the deaths of those in Berdun.

"I hear you ended up being spendthrifts in our shops! Be sure to come back soon with more of your coin!" Captain Torbough laughed.

"With hospitality like yours, I would not miss it," Parner smiled, pointing to the colossal man.

Torbough laughed and smacked both Aten and Parner on the back good-naturedly. Aten stumbled forward extra steps and collapsed into the boat.

"Sorry knight, are you all right?" Captain Torbough asked.

"We have to be careful with Aten on account of his injuries," Gertrude explained, following him on the boat to check if he was okay.

Aten turned to look at her, mortified.

"What is wrong?" she asked.

She turned around and was immediately aware of the amount of eyes on her and Aten in the boat.

The sight was followed by the eerie silence of information being drawn in, the patter of water against the boat was the only thing breaking the silence. Gertrude still did not understand what was wrong until someone spoke up,

"Did you just say Aten?" Captain Torbough asked.

21

The dock stood still for only a moment longer before many things moved simultaneously.

"She did not say Aten, she—" Ren attempted to talk his way out of the situation but he was kicked into the boat by Trise who jumped in after him, drawing her bow and nocking an arrow before she landed. Parner stumbled to get on as well but fell into the water and only hanged on the edge of the boat while Gertrude and Aten sat frozen watching the entirety of the dock move as one collective, arming themselves and pointing at least a dozen bows at the boat.

"One more move and Torbough dies," Trise declared, her bow drawn and pointed at his head.

The men on the dock froze, but Torbough sneered.

"My life means nothing when compared to all of Dervin. Go ahead and kill me, my men will have Aten," he dared.

"Are your men so true in their aim that they would capture him without killing him? Apophis wants him alive," Trise reminded him.

Torbough's smile faltered.

She swayed slightly as Parner began kicking his feet underwater, pushing the boat away from the dock slowly. Gertrude took the cue to slowly grab an oar and help propel the boat while Trise held the bow as steadily as she could. The arrowhead shivered as Trise's strength waned from pulling back the string for longer than the usual breadth's moment before release.

"Does anyone have a shot on the girl? Or a nonlethal one on Aten?" Torbough asked loudly.

Ren stiffened on the floor of the boat. Torbough's men still had not moved from when Trise ordered them to freeze. They looked to one another uncertainly. Gertrude stepped between the dock and Aten, blocking most of their clear sight to him as she rowed further into the lake.

"Answer me!" Torbough commanded.

"No, Captain!" the archers called.

"Apophis will have your heads for this!" Torbough screamed at the boat as Parner and Gertrude struggled to make distance.

"Better ours than his!" Trise yelled, gesturing to Aten.

"You will not be saying that when he has you in his clutches!" Torbough said with conviction.

From there, they were too far from them to hear one another or communicate further. Trise dropped her bow and flexed her arm, grasping at the other oar and rowing with Gertrude.

"Might I get on the boat now?" Parner asked, wheezing from the side of the boat.

Aten realized how exhausted he must have been to be swimming with the armor on and grasped his forearm to drag him out. Parner gasped for a few seconds before looking back to Dervin with concern.

"What do you suppose that is?" he pointed to a watchtower with a large fire lit atop it.

"A signal fire," Gertrude replied, concerned.

"Ah, good. A signal fire that can be seen for miles when there is a dragon searching for us in the skies?" Parner sighed, laying his head against the end of the boat, exhausted.

"We will have to row to our fullest," Trise ordered Gertrude. "And when we tire, we give the oar to one of the knights."

"Right!"

"Who do you think they are signaling?" Aten asked, looking around the lake for any responses to the call.

"It does not matter who they are signaling; they will be upon us as soon as they gather their wits and follow us in their own boats," Trise answered, looking over her shoulder. The dock was rife with activity, but there were no boats after them yet.

Aten took a moment to appreciate everything that had just happened. Trise and Gertrude put themselves in harm's way to save his life. The archers. He did not even mind that Gertrude uttering his name was the cause of the danger, for her actions garnered much of his respect. He looked between the two of them as slowly he realized that, once again, he did not save himself. He was always under the protection of others. He hated himself for it.

"Let me row," he asked, standing suddenly and swaying the boat.

"Aten, your shoulder is in no shape to carry us on the river," Trise said bluntly.

"You did not seem to think that sparring last night was a bad idea!" Aten protested.

"We had no pursuers then," she replied simply.

"I… I order you to!" Aten stammered, desperate to have something to do to repay the people who continued to carry him on his journey.

"No," Trise answered after a moment's internal dissension.

"Gertrude?" Aten said, looking to her with desperation. She did not look at him.

"Aten," Ren said, putting a hand on his shoulder.

"No!" Aten yelled. "They are not on our tails, they are far behind!"

Aten turned back to look at Dervin's shore. Though it was hard to discern individual faces, he could see they were not boarding any vessels. He was also surprised to see that most were not even preparing one to chase after them. Most of them were looking to the sky in many directions.

"Row faster," Aten said, his voice limited.

"What?" Parner said, craning his neck over his shoulder.

Ren stared confused for a moment before his eyes grew wide. He looked to the sky as well, spinning to look in every direction.

"What? What is it?" Parner asked impatiently.

"They are watching the clouds," Ren said, watching them himself.

"Surprised I am not the only one with his head in the clouds?" Parner asked facetiously. He clearly did not understand the problem, so Aten made it clear,

"They are signaling something they expect to come from the sky. They have called the dragon."

22

Trise and Gertrude managed to enter the open mouth of the river leading to Sekoa before they both felt the need to pass the oars to Parner and Ren. Again, Aten attempted to row the boat himself, but was not allowed by the rest of the crew. Parner was still damp from his time in the water, but did not complain about it. They were too busy for that. They collectively watched both the skies and Dervin for any sign of the dragon, but they saw nothing of note thus far as the sun began to dip close to the horizon.

Just a few minutes after they entered the river's mouth, they were out of Dervin's sight, no longer able to keep an eye on any visitors from the sky. The banks of the river were rife with flora, with enough trees along the edge to make the river feel like a corridor taking them to the desert.

"Hang on, why would they be signaling the dragon?" Parner asked a moment after the city was nowhere to be seen. "That does not make any sense. The captain clearly was afraid of it and looked to Apophis to keep them safe."

"Do you think Apophis has ties with the dragon?" Aten asked, coming to the conclusion himself.

The boat looked to him, first incredulously, then with a slow coming to agreement. Gertrude shook her head, refusing to believe it, but the rest began mulling over the idea more seriously.

"That would answer how he could offer protection from the dragon if he controlled the dragon," Parner said.

"It could also explain how he could claim the throne. No matter the size of the army, no dragon would have trouble tipping the balance of power," Ren said.

"Listen to yourselves! Why would the dragon work with a king? What would they have to gain?" Gertrude asked them all. "A dragon could claim the throne himself, if he so chose, so why work with a mere man to play politics?"

"He likes to toy with human affairs?" Parner proposed.

"No, if that were the case, we would have heard about this dragon ages ago. At the very least in legends, much like Vesta was to the rest of the world," Aten said, recalling the woman who sold them the food in Dervin.

"Perhaps the dragon worked with the king to find Aten alive," Trise replied.

Aten stopped to consider it. It felt like it made sense. Assist the king in the coup and get the resources of the kingdom. Then launch a Kingdom-wide hunt. Why be one dragon searching for Aten when the entire kingdom could be ordered to bring him in?

"Clever of you to hide your names so early," Trise mentioned.

"The only name we have heard the dragon utter is 'Aten.' It made sense to hide the one thing he was aware of," Parner replied, basking in the compliment.

Aten thought back to when Parner introduced them with fake names. It had been so seamless, as if he did not have to put thought into it. Aten wished to be more like that.

"Not much has changed, all things considered," Trise thought aloud. "We still search for an answer to defeat the dragon while the dragon searches for Aten, yes?"

The passengers of the boat nodded.

"Good to know our imminent death is not any more imminent than…" Parner stopped talking when he peered at something on the bank of the river up ahead.

"Parner?" Ren asked.

"Do you see the boats? And the outpost?" Parner asked, pointing with his oar.

Aten followed the end of the oar and saw what might have been a boat and a tall, single outpost. Below it was a small clearing, the outpost likely built from trees that used to stand where it stood. He noticed two people on top, but they were too far to tell what direction they were looking. The river carried them closer to the outpost.

"Yes, I see them. What of it?" Aten asked.

"The boats. I believe they are the ones I saw from last night," Parner said, quieting his voice.

Gertrude and Trise drew their bows, nocking arrows and slinging their quivers over their shoulders; their stock of arrows clacking together quietly. Aten drew his own sword and ducked down, not wanting to get in the way of the archer's aim. Ren kneeled next to him, his grip tight on his sword he had not drawn.

"We do not know that they are bandits or raiders, that was only a guess that Gertrude came up with," Ren said. "Perhaps we can talk to them."

"Do you know of this outpost, Trise? Gertrude? Should we expect them to be friendly?" Parner asked.

"I have never been beyond Dervin, myself," Gertrude answered, watching the outpost closely.

"Neither have I," Trise nodded.

"Fantastic, so we are…" Parner stopped abruptly a second time. He drew his sword as quietly as he could.

"The trees," Parner whispered, tilting his head.

Aten squinted and was able to discern a few silhouettes among the trees at the floor of the outpost's clearing. There were more people within them. At least a few dozen. None of them were moving, as if trying to look like branches or trees themselves.

"An ambush," Ren breathed nervously.

"What should we—"

"IT IS HE!!" a voice boomed from on the bank right next to them. "THE BOY ATEN FROM THE SQUARE! HE IS—"

The voice caught when an arrow pierced his windpipe. Aten was barely able to tell where the man was standing before he collapsed dead on the ground. Trise was already nocking another arrow to her bowstring by the time Aten turned to see who fired the shot.

"We have been seen," Trise said quickly, turning to him expectantly.

Aten nodded, spinning to look at Ren and Parner only to see they were looking to him as well. He glanced at Gertrude who was also watching him closely.

"Aten, they are running up the bank, what shall we do?" Ren asked urgently.

Something went awry in Aten's heartbeat. They were looking to him for orders. They never had the luxury of time for orders before, and he never expected to be the one delivering them. His eyes flitted between his people and those running up the river. He analyzed that which he could see from a distance. Sacks being held over shoulders, gleams of swords, light armor on a few bodies, the disarray and tripping of the runners. His instincts went wild.

His mind was brought back to when he confronted Vesta with Tholen's party. He watched them all die. He would not let that happen to his companions. Although it seemed so much led back to Vesta, he would not allow mistakes he made with her to be repeated.

Aten turned to witness a sack being thrown at him before he could decide what should be done.

23

The sack tore open like a cracked melon, revealing a small shower of rocks to fall upon them. It pelted them hard, leaving Aten with stinging pain all over his head, but otherwise no serious injury or damage to the boat.

"Rocks!?" Parner screamed looking at them pile up within the boat. Trise, Gertrude and Ren looked lost, not knowing how to act. Aten looked between the boat and those on the shore.

"Ren!" Aten barked, snapping his fellow knight to attention, "why would they use rocks? Why not arrows?"

Ren was shivering, but his eyes searched the floor for answers. He looked up.

"They fear our archers! They do not want them to be able to focus any shots," Ren replied, his voice quivering.

"Then we do not leave this boat!" Aten ordered. "We remain here and let loose the arrows. Trise! Gertrude! If we are to stand in your way to take the bulk of the blows, would you be able to fire in between us without dealing us harm?"

Gertrude looked uncertain.

"We can," Trise said confidently, drawing her bow and releasing an arrow as soon as she could.

"Quickly! Another hail!" someone from the shore screamed. They heard what sounded like a hailstorm pounding on a rooftop— hundreds of rocks tearing through another sack launched into the air by their assailants.

Aten, Parner, and Ren held their hands over Trise and Gertrude's heads, taking all the hits to defend their archers. Aten felt warm fluid flow down his hands at the end of that attack. Trise let another loose while Gertrude nocked an arrow. They were taking turns to keep their stream of arrows somewhat constant. Gertude's arrow slipped off and she dry fired, the string snapping her forearm mercilessly.

"Focus, Gertrude!" Trise yelled, pulling back her string and releasing another.

"I am trying, but—"

Another shower of rocks fell upon them delaying Gertrude for another moment before releasing. Aten changed a glance over his shoulder to see the numbers of their enemies. There were no more than two scores of them on the shore, with a half-dozen already either killed or too injured to go any further. His eyes lingered on them. They reminded him of the disturbing sight of the fallen Royal Guard of the North.

Some of the attackers were stumbling along, like they were not expecting the battle so soon. Or perhaps they were like him: inexperienced in battle. Others were boarding boats near the outpost tower.

He peered at them, scanning them for their weapons.
All of them were armed with swords, some were
throwing stones from the banks haphazardly, only
about half of them reaching the knights and archers.
He turned his head quickly just before a stone
smashed into him, more fluid leaked down his face.

"Leave us the boy, Aten, and we will let you
live! By order of Apophis!" one of the men atop the
outpost boomed, waving his sword to signal those
below.

Those in the boats pushed off from the banks.
There were three boats, each filled with six men, four
of whom were rowing. Some held rocks in hand even
aboard the boat, waiting to get closer for an easier
throw.

"They are boarding boats! They mean to come
aboard our own and slaughter us with their greater
numbers," Aten thought aloud. Suddenly, a rock
bouncing off his head granted him an epiphany.
"Ren! Is it possible they lack archers? That is why
they have resorted to rocks! We…" Aten realized Ren
stood unresponsive, as if he heard nothing coming
from his mouth. Ren's eyes quivered and his mouth
was drawn to a tight-lipped, terrified frown.

"If they mean to board us then we should row
away instead of allowing ourselves to be carried
downstream to them!" Parner suggested, moving to
pick up an oar. Aten nodded and followed suit. He
noticed his hands were red with his own blood from a

series of small cuts and bruises from the rocks thrown so far. It stung to hold the oar and felt like needles stabbing into his hand when he rowed, his bad shoulder smarting.

"Ren, let us know if you think of anything!" Aten ordered, but saw he still remained frozen, his hands raised slightly in the position to shield Gertrude and Trise from the incoming projectiles.

"Is he in shock!?" Gertrude screamed.

"Use him for cover and continue releasing arrows!" Trise said, kneeling behind him and letting loose another well-aimed shot, taking out another rock-throwing assailant from the banks.

"But he may be hurt!" Gertrude protested.

"Do not focus your gaze on the banks, but those rowing the boats toward us!" Aten ordered the archers. "The men ashore cannot deal us deadly blows, but if those from the boats come aboard, we may not be able to withstand them!"

"Surrender now! You may yet live!" one of the men aboard the boats sang, slapping his sword against the side of his boat in anticipation. They were only about ten boats lengths away from the knights and archers and closing the gap quickly. Not only did they have more men rowing, but they lacked the exhaustion Parner and Aten accumulated on their travel. Aten groaned as he pulled the oar against the water, a mix of his injured arms and the rocks pelting him threatened to be too much for him to bear. He looked at his pursuers and noticed a few bodies in the water behind them. Before Aten could blink, another arrow lodged itself in another man on board, and he was thrown off by the remaining men before one took his place. They were removing literal dead weight in order to catch up.

Gertrude let loose another arrow that whizzed by harmlessly.

"You are no good Gertrude," Aten said, not giving himself time to think of a better way to tell her.

"I am trying!" she cried exasperated. "And what about Ren? What if he is seriously injured?"

"Use the rocks that have made their way on board against the pursuers. If it is a burden to us, then surely it will be a burden to them," Aten told her. He looked at Ren who, while despondent, did not look as though he was seriously injured past the scratches, cuts, and bruises caused by the rocks rained down.

"Let me do it!" Parner volunteered, throwing her the oar and grabbing a handful of rocks immediately. Gertrude nodded and began rowing, their speed increasing considerably with someone more experienced.

Fluid dripped freely from Aten. Whether it was his sweat, blood, or water from the river, he could not tell. He spent all of his energy pushing and pulling the oar as fast and as hard as he could to keep distance from their assailants, who were now less than seven boat lengths away. Trise was superb at marking her targets and continued dropping one after another to the point where they were left with half of what they started with, although their speed waned as Aten's body reached its limit. Parner was able to hit a rower in the eye, slowing them down further with his assault of rocks. Not one boat had enough men to outnumber Aten and his crew. But three assailants together would be enough. And Aten was exhausted to the point of collapse. He looked to Ren and pulled his oar out.

"Aten?" Gertrude asked, her face caked in sweat and bruises.

"Ren, row the boat, all right?" he said quietly as if speaking to a child on the brink of tantrum. Ren's eyes met his and nodded ever so slightly, his hand gripped the oar's handle and unnaturally moved to the end of the boat to row it.

Aten drew his sword and heaved in air, his vision blurry as he held his blade to those closing the gap. He blinked a few times to get a better view of his enemies, but was struck in the face with a rock before anything cleared up. He winced and breathed in deeply.

"You may be brave with your rocks and at a distance, but do you really believe you can exchange blows with a Dragonslayer and live!?" Aten exploded, unable to see if his expressions delivered clearly to his enemies, but seeing oars hesitate mid row.

"We do not need to defeat you! We need only need to bring you to Apophis! The wretched creature of a king wants you alive!" someone responded with false confidence.

"Ha! You think you can take me alive! I will fight to my death!" Aten called to the sky. "I have already won the battle. I will either kill all of you cowards and come out a hero or be slain and come out a martyr!"

Aten's eyes gained clarity and he could see hesitation strewn about the faces of the warriors aboard their boats. Their speed slowed to mere inches of gain on Aten's boat. Even the hail of rocks from the banks halted as well. Aten wobbled a bit, his legs threatening to give out beneath him in his lassitude.

"He is bluffing!" the man who slapped his sword against the boat earlier claimed. "Even if he speaks the truth, Apophis will have our heads if we do not deliver the boy! He will burn us alive, and perhaps all of Arlo as well!"

Aten looked back uncertainly to Ren whom he hoped would be able to talk them out of this situation. But Ren rowed with a vacant expression. Aten noted Trise had another arrow nocked, but was not pulling back on her bow to save her strength.

"We do not wish to fight you," Aten said sincerely, turning back to the men.

"Neither do I, but we have no choice in this matter," the man slapped the boat again and the pursuing rowers picked up their pace once more.

"Perhaps we can negotiate with Apophis!" Parner suggested, rearing his arm back.

"We can only negotiate with the boy in our grasp!" the man said, slapping the boat more anxiously.

"You will die!" Aten said, worried for the man. Trise looked as though she would target him next.

"So be it, you cannot stop Apophis. Even if you are truly a Dragonslayer, Aten. Apophis is a different breed of evil," the man answered.

Aten could not help but look upon the man the same way he saw Tholen the archer. Though this man was in his right mind, he was driven to harm Aten all the same. And he had an army behind him. He sighed, forlorn.

"No point in waiting any longer," Aten nodded to Trise who in turn drew her bow and fired. With that, the rocks came down once more from the banks and those aboard the boats. Aten stood guard in front of Trise, soaking up all the incoming rocks he could.

Trise meticulously took out the remainder of two of the three boats and was aiming for the last one, the man who acted as the leader was still standing, somehow able to avoid Trise's attacks. The man ducked suddenly, avoiding another arrow, then threw a small handful of rocks at Aten's face, blinding him for a moment, long enough for the man to make a mad dive for the boat and land atop Aten, disarming him with a tackle. Aten wasted no time in grappling the man, holding down whatever limb was closest to him.

"Please…" the man whispered to Aten, "Slay Apophis as you did Vesta. You must—"

His throat caught when Parner killed the man, pulling his body off of Aten and helping him up. Aten snapped upward and was overcome by lightheadedness.

"There are no more men on boats," Parner informed him.

"The men on the banks!" Aten said deliriously. "Do not let them flee, for they may let the king know our whereabouts. Gertrude should get her bow and help Trise take them. And we will go to the outpost and kill the men standing at the top."

Aten's vision had gone dark. As the adrenaline faded from his body so did his consciousness.

"And I believe Apophis is—" Aten said, a rock striking his head and knocking him out cold.

24

Aten startled awake at the sound of a crackling fire. At first he thought he was dreaming of the dragon attacking him again, then he felt the wave of pain roll over his body, reminding him of the injuries of the battle. His eyelids cracked open and saw that it was dark out and he was illuminated by a small fire keeping him warm. He was covered by a thin blanket that was purchased from Dervin and looked at the fire when it cracked again. Ren sat at the base of it, his face stone-like.

"Ren—" Aten's voice was dehydrated and sore from screaming. Ren looked up at him and smiled without emotion, picking himself up and placing a waterskin on Aten's chest. Aten took it and consumed the water, stopping only for large gasps of air. He dropped the empty container beside him when finished and took a better look of his surroundings.

Aten sat under the outpost he had seen at a distance. The day had moved to night, but dregs of light still hung over the horizon. At the river, he saw their boat tied to the end as well as a number of arrows protruding from the ground, a collection of evidence of the shots missed by both Gertrude and Trise. Aten noticed a large hole dug near the river and wondered whether it was a grave. His stomach felt nauseous when he realized it was just Ren sitting alone with him.

"Where are Parner and the others?" Aten asked quickly.

Ren put his hands up to calm him.

"They are fine. None of us ended up as injured as you are. Our brother and the archers are burying the dead just beyond the treeline," he pointed. Aten could see torchlight dancing just beyond the first few rows of foliage and relaxed considerably. He laid back down and rubbed his throbbing head, then realizing his hand hurt too much to do that for very long.

"You were quite brave out there, Aten," Ren said, his voice filled with a strange inflection. Aten suddenly remembered that the last time he saw Ren, he could hardly communicate with him.

"Are you all right, Ren? Are you healthy?" Aten asked quickly, straining himself to get up and get a better look at Ren.

"Please, do not get up on my account. Other than a few scratches—none any more serious than your own—I am fine," he assured.

Aten laid back down, keeping his eyes on Ren.

"What happened?" Aten asked simply.

Ren's face morphed into the epitome of shame. His eyes went down and his eyebrows drew close. He picked at a scab on his hand to distract himself. Aten spoke again,

"Ren—"

"Yes, Aten, I know we must speak of it," Ren admitted, embarrassed. He closed his eyes and breathed in deeply. Then, he spoke with finality,

"I am a coward."

Aten frowned and looked at him like he was making a joke.

"You are not a coward?" Aten said, unsure what Ren was trying to get at.

Ren looked at him, imploring him to think on the words.

"Ren, you are not a coward. You are an impressive strategist, one who I have seen react without hesitation in many circumstances. You have successfully maneuvered away from a dragon barrelling toward you with the intent to incinerate you, and have thought on your feet to escape bandits and enemies who hold us hostage. All qualities I wish I had myself," Aten admitted.

"Have you ever seen me in battle, Aten?" Ren asked.

"I..." Aten stopped to think, his eyes closing in consternation. "I suppose I have not. But you looked ready to fight the women of Banti when we were ambushed."

"*Looked*," Ren emphasized, nodding.

Aten shook his head, not truly believing it.

"Ren, you are a knight! How could you be a coward? It is not possible," he said in disbelief. "I have witnessed you deceive our enemies in a moment of peril! Even when we were bound and being dragged as slaves to Berdun, you manipulated the archers aboard the boats!"

"But I did not fight!" Ren said firmly.

Aten's mouth hung open, aghast.

"You are serious?" Aten asked slowly.

Ren frowned, ashamed.

"When I think through things, I do not become so overcome by terror," he explained, his voice quieting. "But when I witness a battle unfolding in front of me…"

Aten thought back to how Ren acted in dire situations. He frowned, unable to think of anything to criticize. Ren ran from a column of flame, but Aten had done the same. He did not show fear when held captive. He cried when witnessing Berdun, as Aten wished he had done as well. It seemed Ren had been in no less battles than himself. He had a hard time wrapping his mind around the idea.

"Ren you assured me you would be with me to the death of the dragon," Aten said.

"And I will stand by my word. I would throw down my life to ensure we will never witness anything like Berdun again," Ren nodded seriously.

"Even if it means a battle with the dragon itself?" Aten asked.

"I expect nothing less to come of this journey," Ren said, shivering slightly.

"Then you are afflicted by something else entirely. A coward would not approach death with such open arms," Aten said, nodding to himself.

"But Aten—"

"Perhaps you have a distaste for taking human lives. It is an honorable disability," Aten declared.

Ren's face went dark in contemplation. His lower lip quivered slightly and he smiled to himself.

"You think too well of me, Dragonslayer," Ren said. "Do you know why those men came after us?"

"Presumably because they heard from Dervin of our escape from them in this direction," Aten shrugged, regretting the movement of his shoulders when they twitched in pain.

"No. I said your name aloud in the center of the square of Arlo when you struck Karn in the face. I am to blame for the injuries caused to us here," Ren said sadly.

"Ah, interesting. Well, it is good to know that we should continue to call me Roth in public, then. Perhaps I need to shed my armor as well if my description is being passed around," Aten said.

"Are… are you not upset?" Ren asked, his face awash with surprise.

"I am upset that they continue to pursue us, I suppose," Aten thought aloud.

"Not, not at our enemies! At me! I am the reason our enemies knew where to find us so soon!" Ren yelled.

Aten watched him carefully. Ren looked how Aten felt when he watched Pallas burn to the ground. He looked full of remorse, and as though he carried all the burdens of the world on his shoulders. Aten smiled compassionately.

"Should I not assume the best of my brother? I am sure you meant no harm, Ren," Aten said sincerely. "In fact, I do not even recall you saying my name in Arlo; are you sure that is what caused them to come here?"

"Yes, I am certain," Ren nodded.

"How can you be so sure? Perhaps the signal fire lit by Dervin was—"

"Because we interrogated one of the men after you lost consciousness. He told us they were sent for us the night after we were ousted. They came to this outpost because we told the woman at the port we intended to go to Sekoa. Their men determined this was the best place to ambush us," Ren explained.

"Ah. I see, and—" Aten ate the rest of the sentence and sat up sharply, most of his body protesting the move. "We captured one alive? Is he still alive? Can I speak with him?"

"Yes, we bound him and left him atop the outpost with nothing more than a cloth to use as a blanket and the clothes on his back. If he tries to flee, he will either have to jump off and kill himself or jump into the water and drown," Ren said.

"Or perhaps he is as adept as you are at escaping from binds," Aten offered.

Ren opened his mouth then closed it in thought, lines creasing across his forehead.

"We should check on him," Ren suggested.

Aten nodded and tried to stand. He stumbled forward, catching himself just before hitting his face on the floor. Ren handed him his sheathed sword to use as a cane and supported his weight under the other arm. Taking steps was excruciating, but not impossible. Aten's body was wracked with pain and fatigue, begging for him to return to sleep, but he needed to speak to the man on the top of the outpost. Ren stopped abruptly at the base of it and shrugged sympathetically.

"We must climb a ladder," Ren said.

"Oh…" Aten said, his face already strained with pain from holding up his body weight. He looked up the length of the ladder. At least five times his height, if not more.

"I can go it alone and relay what he says," Ren offered. "Save your strength, Aten."

"No, I wish to speak to him myself," Aten said, decisively. "You go up first and I will follow by using your leg to pull me up."

Ren shrugged his shoulders and winced, rubbing out a sore in his shoulder before beginning his climb. When he was a few rungs up, Aten gripped onto Ren's boot and used it to pull himself up while he fumbled along the other rungs. It was much easier than he assumed it would be, but he heard Ren breathing heavily in having to also carry his weight. When he reached the top, Ren turned around and pulled Aten up by his good shoulder while Aten fumbled with his legs on the last few rundles.

When pulled to the top, Aten saw a man hunched into a corner with hair disheveled and eyes sunken. Other than scrapes and bruises on his face, his skin looked light pink, burned from the sun. He was bound with rope at both his hands and his feet, with a cloth shoved into his mouth. The man shook his head as Aten approached him slowly.

"You gagged him?" Aten asked.

"I thought he might try to bite through his binds if his teeth were free," Ren explained.

"And the bruises and beatings? Were they there before?"

"Trise did not let up unless he gave us answers to our questions."

Aten looked at him sympathetically. He knew how powerful Trise could be.

"What have you learned?" Aten asked, moving to remove the gag slowly. The man reeled back.

"His name is Hiromoto and he was one of the freshest recruits to Arlo's guards for their docks.

They were visited by King Apophis not long ago and were ordered to bring you in alive, or else they would be killed like those of Berdun. He said they did not want to follow the new king, but were left with little choice between their lives and yours. Apophis is apparently very powerful," Ren said.

"Hiromoto," Aten spoke to the man whose mouth was now free to speak, "you have a strange name."

"I-Yes-I-I am f-from Torn," Hiromoto stammered. He stared at Aten in a mix of terror and awe. "You-You are the Dragonslayer? Dragonslayer Aten?"

Aten felt strange about someone he had never met referring to him this way.

"I am. You are from Torn? Are many of those in Arlo from Torn? What brought you to this Kingdom?"

"No, not many fr-from Torn. I came to Arlo after l-leaving Stanus for a better life. Even th-though most people of Kolog hate us, I thought it-it would be better than l-living in the mountain slums of S-Stanus. I did not know that this land was r-ravaged by a dragon. I n-never would have come," Hiromoto admitted.

"Stanus?" Aten asked.

"A city on the southern end of Torn's Kingdom, just north of Rowa Lake," Ren said from behind him. Aten nodded.

"Very well. Hiromoto, I have a very crucial question to ask you. Did you see Apophis in the flesh?" Aten asked with an energy of anticipation.

The man nodded rapidly, still shivering.

"Is Apophis a dragon?" Aten asked.

Hiromoto's eyes grew wide, his pupils going tight.

"What!" Ren inquired in disbelief.

"N-no, Apophis is ce-certainly a man," Hiromoto answered.

"Describe him to me," Aten said.

"He-he is a man that has a hunched back and a very angry face that looks as though he wishes to tear you apart. His hair-hair is black and he is very strong and knowledgeable. He could fight any one of us. He ch-challenged the dock guards and beat them all wi-without any hint of fatigue. He knew how to start a f-fire in a mere moment. When he arrived he went to one-one corner of the dock with his back turned, and as if by magic, fire appeared," Hiromoto said.

"Aten, do you think…" Ren whispered.

"Did you see his eyes? What were his pupils like?" Aten asked.

"I d-did n-not see them clearly," Hiromoto stammered.

"You said he had a hunched back. Did you see this back of his? What did it look like?" Aten pressed further.

"I did not s-see… He was wearing a cloak. But h-he was tall, even with the back h-hunched o-over. He m-must be severely deformed. When his back was t-turned to us, I-I saw that his hunch looked as though his shoulders were stabbing into his cloak. As if he was hiding angel's wings beneath," Hiromoto relayed.

Aten looked back to Ren whose face was fraught with horror.

"Apophis is the dragon," Ren whispered.

25

"N-no," Hiromoto stuttered, shaking his head.

"It makes sense," Ren explained to Aten. "The reason those cities we have passed are so loyal to him is because they have witnessed his power firsthand. This is not some hearsay of a new king. They have met him! He was ahead of us at every stop!"

"It also explains why they are not allowed to refer to me as Dragonslayer," Aten nodded along.

"And why they never referred to him as a dragon! They simply do not know!" Ren exclaimed.

"N-no," Hiromoto repeated, terrified of the direction of conversation.

"Why would he not come after us himself? Why send the kingdom orders to capture me?" Aten asked.

"Perhaps he was unable to locate us! We slipped from him after fleeing Pallas, and now he has started a manhunt for you," Ren said.

Aten was happy to see Ren back to normal. He may claim to be a coward, but he was a wise companion to converse with.

"Aten?" Gertrude called from the bank of the river.

"We are above!" Aten peeked his head over the side of the outpost. Parner and Trise were with her. In the dim light of the torch they held, Aten could see Parner's eyes were red, and the three of them were covered in dirt. They climbed up the ladder quickly.

"Good to see you awake," Trise said to Aten as soon as she stepped on to the top. Hiromoto pushed himself further into the corner at the sight of her.

"Yes, you frightened me greatly," Gertrude agreed, climbing up behind her.

Parner only nodded, a far off look in his eye. He was there yet unfocused, like something was weighing far more importance in his mind than those in front of him.

"Parner?" Aten asked curiously.

Trise kneeled down next to Aten and whispered.

"He has taken his first life today. It is taking its toll on him."

Aten remembered the nausea and uneasiness he felt at the death of Vesta. He did not know what it would be like to take the life of another man. He nodded compassionately and let him be. Then shook his head of Vesta.

"Apophis is the dragon. Vesta's father," Ren jumped in.

The three newcomers looked at Ren in shock. Then Trise glared at Hiromoto.

"When I asked you to tell me absolutely everything you knew, you failed to mention a dragon!?" she snapped.

Hiromoto cringed and whimpered.

"He did not know," Aten defended.

"Or he lied," Trise said, still glaring at the man.

"No lies! Apophis is no dragon!" Hiromoto insisted.

"How did you determine the king is a dragon?" Gertrude asked.

"Hiromoto described him to us. A man with wings," Aten said.

"A man w-with a hunchback!" Hiromoto corrected.

"And he could create flame in an instant," Ren added.

"With his back turned! Could b-be a trick!" Hiromoto said.

"Is this how dense I sounded when I denied the dragon's existence?" Trise asked Gertrude.

Gertrude bobbed her head side to side in thought, then nodded.

"Hiromoto, have you ever seen a dragon before?" Aten asked.

"N-no, never before. There are no dragons in T-Torn," he stated.

"They look like us. At least the ones I have met," Aten explained. "The most jarring differences are their wings and sharp pupils, like that of a feline. They are also seemingly indestructible, able to destroy weapons that make contact with their skin.

They move impossibly fast, somehow as quickly as an arrow flies from a bow, if not faster."

Hiromoto's eyes went sharp with recognition.

"He did seem to disappear! One moment he was leaving the city on the outskirts of town, then the next moment he was out of sight! None of us could make sense of it in Arlo!" he exclaimed, his frightened stutter replaced by enthusiasm.

"All of you watched him disappear and none of you thought more of it?" Ren asked skeptically.

"It was the dead of night. At that distance it was difficult to see him at all. We were happy he left us after the threats he made to us. And he was able to best anyone in combat who tried to challenge him when he made his decrees. He was not injured at all by the end of it…" he spoke, coming to the realization. "He was a dragon?"

The five, save for Parner, nodded simultaneously. Hiromoto breathed out and let his head hit the frame surrounding the top of the outpost.

"A dragon?" he repeated.

"The one who burned down Pallas and Berdun at that," Trise said.

"And I… I followed its orders to kill you," Hiromoto gazed at Aten. "You killed another dragon so now it seeks revenge?"

"I killed his daughter. And I would say he wants more than revenge. He burned down my homeland and has taken over the throne of the entire kingdom. But he does want to see me dead, I presume. I will defeat him before he gets the chance," Aten said.

"You? You!?" Hiromoto exploded. "You fainted! You passed out in a battle with *men*! The same men who could not leave a scratch on Apophis and you claim to know how to defeat him?"

"I do," Aten said confidently.

Hiromoto watched him carefully. He shook his head, unconvinced.

"Yours is a body prone to injury and fatigue. Apophis was nothing like you. His presence alone was enough to take command of the dock in Arlo. You are… a boy."

Aten tried to shrug, but was held back by his injuries. He was undeterred, regardless. Pirulo would know how to defeat Apophis. He would defeat the dragon.

"What are we going to do with him?" Parner asked, his eyes on the horizon to the south.

The four others looked at Hiromoto whose eyes grew slightly as his lip began to quiver. He pulled against his bindings and inched into the corner even further, squishing himself into the frame.

"Y-you can leave me here. I will not i-inform anyone of your w-whereabouts, I swear! By God, I swear!" Hiromoto insisted, looking terrified at Trise.

"We cannot kill him," Aten acquiesced.

Hiromoto relaxed slightly.

"Why not?" Trise asked.

"We cannot!" Aten said.

"Why? How are we to trust him? We cannot determine what he plans to do from here! Capturing you may be the only thing to protect Arlo from the dragon, what would stop him from coming after us?" Trise asked.

Parner shifted uncomfortably.

"I-I will return to Torn!" Hiromoto declared. "I do not wish to be involved in a land with a dragon!"

"How can we know that?" Trise asked accusatorily.

"I swear by God!" Hiromoto repeated.

"Look at this man," Ren said carefully. "He is completely overcome by fear, Trise. He will say anything he believes will allow him to live."

"Exactly, that is why—"

"That is why we must allow him to leave. He is a man dictated by fear," Ren decided. "He would never want to see us again. Namely Trise. He lost many comrades today and does not look as though he is driven by revenge in any regard. He simply is a man who wishes to live. Whether in Kolog or Torn, I do not care. But he knows if he pursues us, he will die."

The three knights and two archers took time to look over Hiromoto who remained silent, but shivered visibly.

"I agree, we have nothing to fear," Aten said.

"I too wish not to see him harmed," Gertrude said.

Parner nodded.

"I am only trying to finish the order Aten gave before losing consciousness. If he has changed his mind on the matter, then I suppose I will as well," Trise said.

Hiromoto relaxed once more, keeping his eyes on Trise.

"But what will we do with him overnight?" Trise asked, gesturing to the darkness outside. "I do not want him roaming free."

"Very well, we will leave him bound overnight and free him in the morning once we wake," Aten said to the grateful man.

"And we can leave him some of our provisions," Gertude offered.

Trise rolled her eyes at her.

"We do not need to be so merciful to a man that would have killed us only hours ago," she protested.

"Yes, but we have taken much of the provisions of all the men he was once comrades with. I believe that leaving him some of that would be fair, considering I am sure he has claim to some of it," Gertrude said.

"I do not see how that amounts to a 'fair' trade when he would have given us nothing but a sword to the heart," Trise said.

Hiromoto's eyes were flitting between the two women, widening and narrowing rapidly between their arguments.

"Enough," Aten said. "We will do as Gertrude says. Let us go to rest. Someone help me down the ladder please, I will be taking the first watch."

Parner and Ren helped Aten down the ladder from both above and below him while Trise reapplied the gag to Hiromoto. Gertrude made sure it was not too tight as to injure the man. Once on the ground, Ren and Parner insisted Aten should not take a watch tonight, but Aten refused, saying if he was not allowed to take a watch then he would remain awake and watch alongside whoever remained awake. He instead said Parner and Ren should spar if they insisted on forgoing rest. Ren was uninterested and Parner wished to go straight to sleep. When Trise and Gertrude came down, Trise told Gertrude they would practice with their bows and arrows in the morning before wishing Aten a good watch.

Aten watched the river flow in the dim light left by the remaining embers of the fire. His arms throbbed and his legs begged to be put to sleep, but he endured, only to feel like he had done something for his group. Even in battle, he could not accomplish much but talk. He did little in terms of combat. It formed a pit in the frustration building within him. Days ago, he thought archers were scum, but today he relied on them to save his life. He felt the only thing he contributed to his comrades was killing Vesta, and he was alone then. He shook his head impatiently.

All things led back to Vesta.

He watched the sky closely and wondered if Apophis ever made his way to Dervin by the signal fire. He also wondered whether anyone from Dervin was on their tail. He was both calm and anxious watching the water that came from Dervin. He had no way of knowing if anything would be coming and how high of alert he should be on. It was an eerie calm that the river carried.

Aten heard one of his comrades stir behind him. He wondered if it would be easy to fall asleep after today's battle. He felt he could be in slumber the moment his head touched the ground. He had been that tired for a long time now. But he also wondered if he would be meeting Vesta and Apophis in his dreams once again. He thought the latter to be likely.

Footsteps approached him from behind. Parner sighed and sat next to him, watching the water.

"Go to sleep, Parner," Aten suggested quietly.

"I cannot," Parner whispered with such confidence that Aten knew not to try to suggest it again.

They sat staring at the water for a few minutes, enjoying the company of each other's silence.

"What was it like—that is what did you feel—when you killed Vesta?" Parner asked.

Aten thought about it seriously.

"It was both exhilarating and a moment of immediate regret. I did not know whether what I had done was just. It took me some time to come to terms with what I had done. I am still uncertain whether I had done the right thing now that Apophis ravages the land in her place, but I have come to terms that it was necessary."

Parner nodded.

"Thank you, Aten. You led us well today. I thought us dead. If not all of us, at the very least one of us. The rocks were such a surprise that I lost all forms of intelligent thought," Parner expressed.

"I did nothing but stand in the way of the rocks," Aten shook his head.

"Did nothing? Aten, we would not be here were it not for you. Did you not see us? We were lost," Parner whispered loudly. "You led us to victory. We owe our lives to you."

"We owe our lives to Trise and Gertrude. The very archers I once loathed," Aten deflected.

"And they owe their lives to us because we stood in the way of the rocks and for that we owe our lives to you for giving us the order. Do you remember at the guild? We were once instructed to do something very important whenever three or more of us traveled in a group. Do you know what we were told to do?"

"Assign a leader?" Aten recalled. Parner nodded.

"I see the wisdom in that now. While it may have been by your knowledge of dragons before, I think you are the best leader for us. The one that unites us by both your Pallas blood and for being Dragonslayer Aten."

Aten had never thought that there was wisdom behind that instruction before. But now he could not think of a group he met on this journey that did not have a leader. Banti had Trise. The guild had Boros. The Royal Guard of the North had Captain Brun. Even Tholen's men followed his lead. It released some of the tension building within him. Perhaps he had done something for this group after all. He was a leader.

Just as he had gained comfort in that fact, he saw the silhouette of something cross the sky rapidly in the direction of Dervin. Whether it was Apophis or some other creature of the night, Aten did not know.

26

Aten was roused gently by Gertrude, who placed a slab of rock on the ground then put a piece of meat and potatoes atop it as soon as his eyes cracked open. He rubbed the tire from his eyes and willed the previous night's dream to leave him. The dragon Apophis sat upon a throne with a crown on his head, blaming Aten for the destruction of Kolog. It did not sit well with him.

"I apologize, but we have nothing in the form of plates, so I cleaned some flat rocks to eat from," Gertrude said quickly. She seemed to be in a hurry.

"Are you going somewhere?" Aten asked, looking around drowsily. Ren and Parner at at the water's edge enjoying the meal while Trise stood under the outpost looking seemingly impatient.

"Trise insisted on practicing with the bow this morning. I apologize if you wanted to leave sooner, but she is very adamant about this," Gertrude said apologetically.

As Aten's focus returned to reality, so did the pain of hundreds of rocks of yesterday's battle. He strained to sit up and would not have been able to do it had Gertrude not pulled him up gingerly.

"Do what you feel is best. Just let Hiromoto go before we forget," Aten said, rubbing his temple to nurse an oncoming headache.

"We already released him."

"Ah, I am glad you let him off early."

"Aten, it is well past midday."

Aten blinked a few times and looked up to see the sun beyond its zenith. He blinked a few times more to understand just how long he had been asleep.

"I take it you tried to wake me?" Aten asked.

"At least for breakfast, yes. Now hurry and eat your lunch so you can regain your strength," Gertrude pushed the rock slab closer to him and stood. She moved briskly to Trise who led her to a tree with a makeshift target on it.

Aten ate in silence, examining his arms in the sunlight. They were mostly covered in bruises, though also wracked with small, shallow cuts. He flexed his forearm and felt a litany of aches and pains surge through him. It would be difficult to pick himself off the floor, let alone carry a sword. He wondered when he would truly be able to rest.

Ren turned and smiled when he saw Aten awake, nudging Parner. Parner winced at being nudged and punched Ren back. Aten laughed as Ren howled in pain and shoved Parner over before running to Aten's side.

"Welcome back," Ren said.

"I think you slept enough for all of us given the time you took," Parner caught up.

"If it is so late in the day, why are Trise and Gertrude just beginning to practice?" Aten asked.

"They have been loosing arrows into trees all day. Trise has been yelling into her ear the entire time to ensure she can focus under pressure the next time the need for their skills arises," Ren explained.

"Is it benefitting her?"

"I doubt we will know until we need to," Ren said.

"And you two? Have you been sparring?" Aten asked.

Ren and Parner looked to one another, embarrassed.

"We mostly took count of our new inventory and planned our way to Sekoa," Parner said.

"You took a break," Aten concluded.

The two nodded in agreement.

"I think... I think Ren might benefit from the same kind of training as Gertrude," Aten suggested, not meeting Ren's eyes. The sound of Trise's orders and beratement made its way to the knights.

"I can spar with you all without a problem," Ren said defensively. "It is fighting the unknown that I am not prepared for."

"And I do not need any such practice, seeing how I was able to kill someone *without* needing them to fall in love with me," Parner said mischievously.

Aten grinned. He was happy to see Parner back to his usual self. He was also pleased to see that Ren knew where his weaknesses lied. He wondered where his own were for a moment before another wave of pain flowed through his aching body.

"When can we be off?" Aten asked, digging into his meal of meat and potatoes.

"We are prepared to disembark at a moment's notice. Trise has been especially focused on Gertrude, to the point where she ignores us," Parner said with a hint of chagrin.

"Perhaps she will listen to you," Ren suggested.

Aten looked to the archer's mid-chew. If he was strong enough to stand on his own, he decided, he was strong enough to leave. He swallowed his morsel of food and braced himself. He groaned and arduously dragged his feet under him to pick himself up. Ren and Parner moved to assist him, but he held his hands up to signal them back. He groaned once more and fought the flames of pain burning brightly in his legs, moreso in his injured calf. With a misstep catching himself forward, he was able to stand upright.

"Amazing," Parner said sarcastically. "Simply witnessing you stand up may be enough to defeat the dragon by sheer intimidation."

"Shut up, Parner."

Aten used the sheath of his sword to hobble over to the archers, the intense training led by Trise grew more intimidating as he drew nearer. Aten could see Gertrude wearing something over her forearm today to protect from the string snapping at it. He wondered whether they had that yesterday and if they did not have the time to put in on. Soon, he was close enough to hear Trise's lesson.

"Again! Walk and shoot the target! Sometimes you and your opponent are in motion. Are you going to let them get the advantage? Are you?"

Instead of replying, Gertrude shot at the tree. A near-miss from the center. Aten was impressed, but Trise scoffed.

"If your enemy's helmet is tight, you will not have the luxury of missing by massive margins like that. Again!"

"Trise! Gertrude!" Aten cut in awkwardly. "We should be going."

Trise looked him up and down for a moment, her energy dissipating.

"You are well enough to travel?" she asked, a red hue fading from her face.

"Well enough to want to travel."

Trise shrugged and tilted her head at Gertrude to gather the arrows. Aten made his way back to the boat, his bad leg buckling every few steps, but he tried to keep that a secret from the others. He could sit and rest on the boat. He would not volunteer to row. Parner and Ren helped Aten step aboard and the four of his companions gathered their supplies and pushed off into the river. Trise and Gertrude began rowing gently.

"I can row," Parner offered.

"Take a look at your hands," Trise responded.

He looked down at the litany of scratches, welts, and scabs threatening to tear open.

"I will be fine."

"You will be better off when you let your hands rest for the day," Gertrude replied.

"We must at least attempt to repay your bravery yesterday. The three of you did well to act as cover when we were under the rock rain," Trise said.

Ren stiffened, embarrassed, but Parner chuckled.

"We have had fire rain down upon us, as well as rocks. I feel as though we will experience a rain of air before a natural rain of water," he said, amused.

"A rain of air?" Trise challenged.

"I would have asked you what a rain of fire or rocks were only a fortnight ago! Do not consider it out of the question," Parner laughed.

Aten was happy at both the speed they went at and the calmness they enjoyed this day. He was grateful for both the provisions they had and the company he kept. As his wounds took their time to heal, he was pleased to make more headway to the Deserted Desert. Soon, he would be able to defeat Apophis.

The borders of the river gave way to less trees and more plains the further they drifted south. Hours, they went with casual, short conversation or just relishing the silent journey south. The knights would routinely readjust themselves to take pressure off of one point of pain only to inevitably agitate another sore when they sat back down. Aten could see rolling hills out in the distance on his right. He squinted at them for a moment.

"Do the hills look… unnatural?" Aten asked. Parner scoffed.

"What a question! Do the hills…" Parner frowned mid-sentence. "They do look a bit unnatural, do they not?"

The hills were a dark black, as if covered in a thin sheet of tar. There was no foliage to be seen anywhere near them, and a light scent of something burning hung in the air.

"This is where Apophis stopped…" Ren said in an abated breath.

"Stopped?" Gertrude asked.

"We are east of Pallas. The dragon chased us this way, razing the land as it flew. It left nothing but scorched earth in its wake. It seems this is where it decided to look for other means of finding Aten," Ren said.

Aten looked closer at the hills. They did not look familiar, but it was possible that the tiremarks of the wagon they took from Waron would be found within the carnage, or perhaps the wagon itself. Aten wished he could return it to the weaponsmith, but he knew it was unlikely he would find anything in the ashen terrain. He watched the hills intently, imagining the white, hot flames bearing down on them and leaving them in the state they were. He could follow a line, a scar written in the ground by fire that made a trail all the way back to Pallas. He felt a renewed drive to find Pirulo. He never wanted to see this kind of large-scale destruction again in his life.

"This is the power Apophis possesses?" Trise asked in awe.

"You act like you did not witness Berdun," Parner replied.

"I just… I thought it was more limited in its ability to produce fire. How do we defeat a monster like this?"

"We find someone who already knows how," Aten answered confidently.

Ren looked to him skeptically, but the others nodded in agreement. Aten's gaze fell back on the river when his jaw dropped at the site ahead of them.

A giant tree, taller than anything he had ever seen, loomed ahead, its branches comparable to clouds in their size above a small city and lake at its base. Beyond the tree, on the horizon, Aten could see a desert, but the tree took command of the view, probably visible for miles around.

"What is that!" Aten pointed, his arm stinging in protest.

The other passengers followed his gaze, then followed his expression, all of them looking in wonder. Ren suddenly perked up and went into one of the bags onboard. He pulled out a parchment with detailed images scrawled across it.

"I witnessed it on the map, but believed it an exaggeration," he said, pointing and showing the group the parchment was a map. "That is the tree towering over Sekoa. We have arrived!"

Aten looked at the map, then at the city. Ren was right in that it looked comically large for a tree on the map, but it truly was a sight to behold.

"What a marvel," Aten said.

"I have heard tell of this tree before," Parner said. "I believe it is called a Sekoa Tree, named after the city or perhaps the other way around. Legend says that the entire city was built from the branches pruned from this fantastic feat of foliage."

"Fantastic feat of foliage?" Trise smirked.

"I am as erudite as I am loquacious," Parner said pompously, bowing.

Aten recalled that 'loquacious' was a word that Vesta had once used. He still did not know what it meant, but chuckled at Parner's display, regardless. He was in high spirits. He felt their journey would be ending soon.

27

Sekoa was a city built on one end of the lake with the Sekoa Tree towering over them on the other side. It was able to shade the entire city with its massive branches, the leaves allowing a gentle sprinkle of sunlight to make its way across the town, as if a massive basket weaved over the entire city. Further into the lake, Aten could see the edge of what looked like a waterfall that fell right into the Deserted Desert from a steep cliff. Listening closely, he could make out the distant roar of the falls, and wondered whether there was anything on the bottom that resembled the oasis Pirulo lived in. He was thrilled at the thought of Pirulo being so close now.

Their boat did not have a dock to be placed in as each home seemed to have a boat of their own next to their residence. Trise and Gertrude made their way between many others rowing their boats, mostly to and from the great tree on the other side of the lake; those coming in had piles of wood stacked into their boats.

As deftly as they rowed, Aten's group's boat kept receiving odd stares from the Sekoan residents. Aten had stripped off his knight's armor in hopes to remain in disguise and looked little more than an infirm young man who had been beaten badly. He wondered if that was why they were being watched.

Trise and Gertrude located a spot to stop the boat just off the end of one side of Sekoa, tying their boat to a boulder. Aten looked at the banks and could not help but be surprised by how barren it all was, as if life had been stripped away from everything here but the Sekoa tree. He was able to lift himself up and climb out of the boat on his own despite his injuries, having had ample rest during the trek to the lakeside village. He looked out to Sekoa, astounded by the architecture of the buildings.

They were all intricately crafted, each with their own unique flair as if all built by a different designer. They all looked sturdy, built from strong wood as opposed to the old mix of material used in Pallas. Aten looked back at the massive tree looking down on him and wondered if it was truly possible to gather enough material from it to build these residences without any scars across the face of the tree trunk.

"I can already feel the desert heat," Parner complained fanning his face.

"It is worse within," Aten warned him.

"Do you believe Parner's head can get any hotter?" Ren asked with faux concern.

Aten's chuckle was stopped abruptly by the scorn on someone's face only ten paces away, next to one of the houses they placed their boat next to. It was a woman who scowled at them sourly and spat at their feet before asking,

"Outsider, eh?"

"Who said we are outsiders? It is a large city after all," Ren stepped forward immediately.

The women shifted an eyebrow toward their boat.

"That is not made of Sekoa wood," she answered simply.

Aten looked back at their boat and at other passerbys in the water. He could not tell the difference in wood make-up. Those floating by were still staring at the boat as they passed. Evidently, they could tell it was foreign just as easily as this woman.

"And what of it?" Ren asked. "What if we made our boat of other material?"

"Then you are an outsider."

"We are outsiders. What of it?" Ren admitted.

"What do you filthy outsiders want with our Sekoa?" she asked, mildly infuriated.

"The town? We only intend to pass through," Ren answered placatingly.

"The town? No! Our tree! What do you want with it?" she repeated, slightly assuaged.

Ren tilted his head, not understanding the question. Gertrude spoke up gently,

"Nothing. We intend to spend the night in this hospitable town and then travel into the desert."

The woman scrunched her face.

"You will take the cripple to the Deserted Desert?" she asked skeptically gesturing to Aten with another flick of her brow.

"The 'cripple' will *lead* them into the desert," Aten answered indignantly.

The woman eyed them all closely.

"You have money?" she asked suddenly.

Trise shook a pocket, the jingle of coins shimmering out and braced herself to fight. Rather than say anything more in revulsion, the woman's scowl turned to a bright smile in a fluid motion, her teeth shining excitedly.

"Lovely to meet wondrous outsiders! I am Fera! Do you require a place to stay? An inn? Perhaps a safe place to store your vessel?"

Aten was stunned by her turn in both expression and tone. He looked to Parner who was very amused by this development and grinning wildly. He chuckled as Ren continued conversing with her.

"We are no longer filthy outsiders?" Ren asked cautiously, not wanting to upset her once more.

"Filthy? Ha!" she laughed goodnaturedly, "I am sure I said something otherwise. You are esteemed guests to Sekoa! Please, come with me, I can show you a place to stay and store your vessel along the waterline."

"Actually, we are looking to sell the vessel now that we have arrived. We are no longer in need of it if the next step in our journey is to enter the desert," Ren explained.

"Of course, of course," Fera said, encouraging the group to follow her as she went to untie the boat and pull it along with them. She remained along the edge of the water, beaming the entire time and smiling to the group at intervals of a few steps. If Aten had seen her like this at first, he would have never believed she had the ability to scowl. It made him think there were other types of deceit he was not yet familiar with. A less hostile form of deceit that could still prove useful.

"Some outsiders are absolutely filthy, are they not?" Parner pushed past Ren to speak to the woman pulling their boat and supplies.

"Oh yes," she nodded without an ounce of malice. "Some have been known to visit us only to take our livelihood." She raised the rope to point to the Sekoa Tree across the lake.

"The tree pays your wages?" Parner asked, smiling.

"Nothing can grow in this city," Fera answered unperturbed, kicking the barren earth lightly. "We cannot make our own food, and the fish of the lake are very few. Whether it be our nearness to the desert, or perhaps the Sekoa Tree's roots stretching this far, we cannot farm any crop on the earth. Rather, we harvest the fallen branches, or branches deemed worthy of trimming from the great tree. We have our artisans create great works from them such as wagons for passing merchants or homes for ourselves, and sell the wood for its high quality."

"Surely you do not mean to say the tree dispenses enough material for the entire town to have enough money by these means?" Trise asked.

"Not all of us. A few are fisherman, others seamstresses, and a few gather rare specimens from the desert to sell to the merchants. But the vast majority are heavily reliant on the Sekoa," she said with deference.

Aten looked back up to it, craning his stinging neck as far back as it would allow to try and get the entire tree in view. His mouth was open, totally in awe of the ability of one tree to be the source of all shelter and trade in the area. The city simply would not exist without it. He felt the respect that Fera had for it. The tree was the opposite of a dragon.

"Every building in Sekoa is made of the tree, then?" Parner asked.

"Not just Sekoa," Fera said, impassioned. "The village of Pallas was made mostly of Sekoa, God rest their souls. Kit and Merdo have a few key buildings made from Sekoa, as well. And Kolog! I would say half the capital has a touch of Sekoa to it!"

"If you are able to supply so much of the kingdom with this material, why would it matter if an outsider would like to enjoy it as well?" Ren asked.

Fera shook her head as she walked, she stopped the boat in front of a larger building along the water, tying it to a stake planted into the earth right outside the door of the building. She was able to knot it in a moment, as if having practiced it so often that she did not even have to think to succeed.

"Outsiders do not understand the delicate balance we have with the Sekoa Tree," Fera said sadly. "We can take from those that fall, yes, but of the branches we prune, we are very careful. We want the Sekoa to thrive for generations beyond our own. We could easily cut down the entire tree and sell the wood for a fortune, but what of our children or grandchildren? They would be forced to leave this town when there is nothing that will grow and they have nothing to sell. The outsiders have never wanted less than that which will make them large swaths of money. As if they intend to swim in their riches and drown in them. Their greed has led to many difficult years for the Sekoa, and therefore to our city. Even the magician Apophis took from our wealth, likely wanting to bolster his already unattainable wealth as King. Outsiders cannot accept God's bounty except to ask for more. We no longer allow them on the other side of the lake."

Aten took another look to the far side of the water. He would not be allowed to walk there. A land he would be an enemy for stepping into. Like Arlo and Dervin. Aten felt his safe havens slipping through his fingers like the sand of the desert.

"The *magician* Apophis?" Ren asked, interested.

"He simply appeared to declare himself King, took from the tree, and vanished, as if in thin air. I have no idea how a man could do such a thing except that he was a magician," Fera shrugged.

Aten felt a chill run down his spine at the idea that Apophis had already been here. Somehow the dragon was simultaneously a step ahead and creeping behind him at all times. It was maddening.

"Top!" Fera snapped a finger at the building. "We have visitors!"

The door to the building flung open and a bald man wearing a necklace of wood stepped out, beaming.

"Visitors! I love outsiders!" he boasted, showing his teeth. Aten was stunned to see one was made of wood.

"They wish to sell the boat," Fera pulled at the string she tied. Top's eyes narrowed on it for a fraction of a moment before he turned to the group.

"One silver!" Top said, pulling a coin from his pocket and presenting it grandly.

"One!?" Trise balked. "This vessel brought us here from Banti as is in fine condition!"

"A boat not made of Sekoa wood is already substandard!" he said, stepping out of the doorway and walking down to the water's edge to point to pieces on the boat. "But it is not only of substandard material, but it is also chipped up and down, as if you traveled through a hailstorm through Rowa Lake to get here!"

Top was pointing to many chipped pieces of wood that were as a result of the rain of rocks from the ambush at the outpost on their way here. The group was unable to answer for those.

"And now that I am here, it seems to have a hint of the smell of burnt wood. As if you have set fire to this? Or perhaps set it too close to a campfire?"

It never occurred to Aten that the soot of Berdun could have made its way here, but he never picked up on the scent before. This man smelled it the moment he approached it.

"Were I not a man of my word, I would reduce my price to nine bronze, but I already led with the silver and will not reduce," Top said, spinning on his heel to look at the group. Evidently, they were as stunned as Aten, for none of them spoke. Top laughed and flicked the coin into Trise's hand.

"A deal!" Top said confidently.

"Yes," Trise said, confused. She pocketed the coin and helped Parner and Ren gather their belongings from the boat that no longer belonged to them.

"All of you will be staying the night, I take it? Perhaps more? The crippled one looks as though he is done with travel," Top pointed a thumb at Aten.

"Actually, the cripple intends to take them through the desert soon!" Fera answered.

"I would kindly ask the both of you not to refer to me as 'the cripple,'" Aten said through clenched teeth.

Top's eyebrows rose to his forehead and he inched deftly to Fera.

"The cripple seems to be in denial," Top whispered loudly to her.

"Then what are we supposed to call him?" Fera whispered back, exasperated.

"Roth is fine," Aten answered her.

The two of them looked stunned at his response.

"Roth the Cripple seems to be quite adept at hearing us," Top whispered loudly.

"No," Aten yelled, "I—"

"How much does it cost to stay the night?" Ren asked quickly. Aten frowned, but willed himself to calm down.

"Five bronze per bed per night," Top replied, counting them up. "Which would come out to two silver and five bronze. I can get you all in two rooms. One with two beds and one with three beds."

"Excellent," Parner nodded. "Ren and Roth in one room and the rest of us in the other."

Parner was met with blank stares.

"I thought it was funny," Parner shrugged.

"It was not," Trise replied. Parner flushed with shame.

"If I am to give you a gold coin, will you give us a cooked meal in the morning as well as keep our identities a secret?" Trise flashed the money.

Fera smiled her amiable smile while nodding and Top laughed.

"I will keep your identities so secret, I will not learn them myself!" he snatched the coin from her hand and opened the door wide for them to enter the inn.

28

Aten, Ren, and Parner had settled into their room for the night, the three of them sitting at the edge of their bed at odd angles to best accommodate the wounds and bruises from the trip thus far. Trise and Gertrude bid them an early goodnight and turned into their rooms across the hall. Parner was bouncing lightly on the cot, looking around the room excitedly.

"I cannot remember the last time I slept in a bed," he sighed contentedly.

"What is our plan, then?" Ren asked.

"We enter the desert tomorrow if my wounds allow. We will find Pirulo, then kill Apophis and avenge Pallas," Aten said, determined.

"And how would we go about finding Apophis?"

"Come now, Ren. That is simple!" Parner said. "We request an audience with the king in the capital city of Kolog!"

Aten was still thinking about the question when Parner delivered the answer. They would go willingly to the capital city in order to find the dragon? He could not think of a better plan. He would still require the element of surprise to defeat Vesta's father, that he was sure of.

"You think we would be able to set foot in Kolog?" Ren scoffed.

"Better that we have to travel there rather than the Kingdom of Torn," Parner pointed out.

"We cannot travel to Torn?" Aten asked, curious. "I know of their hostilities as a kingdom to our own, but admit I do not know much more in terms of their actions as a whole."

Ren scratched his chin thoughtfully.

"I must admit I have never stepped foot in the Kingdom of Torn, myself. Perhaps they are not as aggressive to Kolog as we believe," he thought aloud.

"Or perhaps they are much worse!" Parner said helpfully.

"But what are these assumptions?" Aten clarified.

"I was told that they would bind us and force us into slavery as soon as they discovered we were from Kolog. We would be forced to help their army in their preparations to invade Kolog," Ren said.

"And I was told we would simply be tortured gratuitously then killed on sight. If you are dead it means you cannot sabotage the men in the invasion force," Parner said.

"And Kolog?" Aten asked. "Do we not harbor the same hostilities toward those of Torn?"

"We have seen a few come to our kingdom, similar to Hiromoto. I have never known us to harm them, but we do not treat them particularly well," Ren said.

"Yes, I would much rather be from Torn in Kolog rather than the other way around. I was essentially told Torn harbors so much ill will toward us that even to step foot in their kingdom as someone from Kolog would brand you a dead man and a fool," Parner said.

"It would make sense if they intend to invade our land," Ren agreed.

"Is there any evidence they intend to invade our lands?" Aten asked.

Both knights shrugged. Aten wondered where the truth of the matter lied.

"Regardless," Ren continued, "do either of you believe we can enter the capital and kill this dragon? Surely our descriptions have made our way back to the king by now. Even our false names likely require more work. I fear we may be captured or killed prior to our confrontation with the beast, and that is assuming we will even have the means to defeat him by then."

"Not to mention that it seems the dragon burns down villages anytime it becomes impatient in its search for…" Parner did not want to say Aten's name and simply gestured to him.

"I have slain a dragon before. Alone. With you by my side, I am certain we will be able to achieve this again," Aten whispered confidently. He laid back on his bed, his wounds cherishing their time of rest.

"Very well," Ren said begrudgingly. "I suppose there is no better plan than to go to the desert, find Pirulo, and kill the dragon."

"If we had gone there from the beginning we could have saved ourselves all these arduous days of travel," Parner yawned.

"How do you mean?"

Parner pointed to Aten.

"He first mentioned Pirulo when we left Pallas. If we had simply ran South instead of East, we very well could have defeated the beast by now."

"Or we could have been spotted and killed by a dragon spitting a wall of fire below him," Aten answered, his eyes closed and his head on a pillow.

"I like to think we would have made it if we were able to get this far," Parner said.

Aten heard Ren begin to reply, but was drifting into sleep and did not make out what he said.

Aten stood before Vesta Forest, the entire treeline engulfed in white flames. For once, he immediately knew he was in a dream. Apophis was somewhere in the forest, likely on his way out.

"You cannot defeat him without me, you know," a voice appeared next to him. He turned his head to see Vesta, her thin pupils watching the fire spread before them.

"You are dead," Aten said to her, unsure if she was aware.

She shrugged noncommittally.

An explosion bloomed overhead as an enraged roar emerged from within the forest. Aten braced himself and lifted his dagger, only to see it was a hilt with a broken blade.

"Aten!!" Apophis's face broke through the trees followed by a blast of flame overwhelming both him and Vesta.

Aten woke with a start, a strand of sunlight that made its way through the Sekoa's shade warming his body through a small window in the room. He rolled onto his side, disappointed. He disliked that Apophis followed him both in dreams and reality.

29

Aten took his time to flex his muscles and feel for sores and pangs as he looked around the room. Ren was still asleep Parner was peering out the window intently. Aten was happy to find that the litany of pains of the day before were dulled now, only flaring when pressed on by his fingers. He may be able to travel today.

"You are up early," Aten yawned to Parner. "Taking watch by looking out the window?" he joked.

"I was thinking about someone," Parner answered, sounding as though his mind was not quite in the room.

"Who?" Aten asked.

"Who?" Parner asked, his focus returned. "No one. I said something. I was thinking about something," he corrected, his face a hint of pink.

"And what were you thinking about?" Aten asked.

"Err… I was thinking about what time we should expect the food," Parner answered quickly.

"Always on your mind, eh?" Aten joked.

Parner eyed him, as if not convinced that they were really talking about food. Aten eyed him back.

"The townspeople mention you," Parner gestured out the window, his voice clearly wanting to jump to a new topic of conversation.

"They know of me?" Aten asked incredulously.

"They say King Apophis has done nothing in his new position of rule except to offer grand wealth to those that capture you alive. And the destruction of the town of those that bring you in dead."

"Who said this?" Aten asked cautiously.

"I pieced it together from listening to those on the way to the lake in the morning. I wonder what Apophis would do if I brought your dead body to Kolog. Do you think the dragon would burn down Pallas a second time?" Parner smiled mischievously.

"That is no way to lead a kingdom. Much could be solved with the Kolog's riches," Aten said, shaking his head.

Parner guffawed, causing Ren to stir in bed.

"The king has burned down two villages—that we know of—and you are concerned with the kingdom's finances?" Parner asked.

Aten's face went red in embarrassment as a knock came to the door.

"We heard Parner's laughter," Gertrude's voice came through. "Breakfast is ready if you are all awake."

Parner picked up the end of Ren's blanket and tore it off of him quickly. Ren raised his whole body in protest, the space under his eyes covered in light wrinkles.

"Give it back," Ren yawned.

"We are all awake!" Parner called back to the door jovially, tossing Ren his blanket back and telling him, "Get up quickly, breakfast will get cold before you get there!"

Aten stumbled after him, his legs smarting with pain, but nothing serious enough to slow him down. Outside their room and down the hall was a modest room with two tables. One was occupied by Trise and Gertrude, while the other remained empty. Fera was placing another helping of food on the table as Aten entered. She smiled at him and went back to the scents of the kitchen.

"Did you sleep well?" Gertrude asked between bites.

"Better than I deserve," Aten nodded. Gertrude looked worried.

"It is how he says 'yes,'" Parner explained, allaying her.

"Ah! The knight is up! And the other one," Top nodded to Parner and Aten respectively as he entered the building. "You two sleep like rocks. These two were practicing their archery from the early morn. The angry one is quite adept."

Trise looked up to acknowledge the compliment, but kept her focus on her food.

"You know," Top lowered his voice approaching the table. "Outsiders came asking for some knights. One by the name of 'Aten.'"

Aten froze, his hand hovering over a warm piece of bread.

"What did you tell them?" Aten swallowed.

"I told them we had a cripple if that interested them!" Top quipped loudly. "They went off without any more questions!" he laughed, showing off his wooden tooth and making his way into the kitchen. Aten rolled his eyes, annoyed.

"Wait!" Aten called him. Top turned to him. "What did they look like?"

"A man with a fresh burn on his hands was the one of spoke to me. The others behind him were armed and armored. They seemed organized, and were certainly outsiders by their garb and lack of any Sekoan mannerisms." Top entered the kitchen, assisting Fera with breakfast.

"Are you well?" Trise asked Aten after swallowing a mouthful of water.

"I am not as weak as Top insists on describing me," Aten offered.

"I am also well," Parner interjected, smiling to Trise.

"I mean to ask are we entering the desert today?" Trise clarified.

Aten felt around his arms and legs a few times, taking special note of the pain in his calf from the wound dealt to him by Tholen, the archer.

"I believe I am well enough to travel today. And it seems we have no time to waste. Someone is here in search of us," Aten said.

Ren groggily pulled himself to the table, smacking his lips as he grabbed a piece of bread and some bits of meat, his other hand holding loosely to a parchment.

"Who is in search of us?" Ren asked aimlessly, taking a bite of the bread.

"Dervin has caught up to us," Parner said.

"We do not know that it is those same men. It seems they are not led by Torbough. I think his most telling attribute would have been his size, but Top said his hands were burned," Trise said.

"That is true," Parner corrected himself quickly, looking at Trise for approval, "we are not sure of the nature of these men. Perhaps they have heard of the reward put out by the king and are simply working on their own accord."

"I do not think it matters," Aten said. "We should be discreet and enter the desert regardless of the origins of these pursuers."

Ren flattened a parchment on the table. It was the map he had purchased from Dervin. He looked at it closely, Parner looking over his shoulder.

"There has to be an opening to the Deserted Desert that does not involve jumping off the cliff," Ren said, running a finger lightly over the map.

"It says that there is a path that goes from here to Pallas," Parner pointed out.

"That is the opposite direction of where we need to go," Ren looked at him.

"Yes, but Aten entered the desert from Pallas. This desert is massive," Parner waved his hand over the map, "it may be that the bard lives nearer to Pallas than elsewhere."

The two knights looked up to Aten who shrugged mid-bite.

"I do not recall where I was or which direction I went to find Pirulo," he said, his mouth full of food.

"Very well, how did you end up finding the lutenist?" Trise asked.

Aten shrugged again.

"The elders of Pallas told me that those with open ears would find the secrets of the desert. I closed my eyes and left my ears open," he explained.

Trise's eyes grew wide. Ren and Parner dropped the food they were holding.

"You do not know where you went?" Trise asked loudly.

"Aten, you waited until now to tell us this information?" Ren asked, looking at the map more worriedly than before.

N. T. Lazer

"Be kind, Aten has been through so much on this journey," Gertrude said, trying to calm them down.

"Ah, yes, and I have had just the most wonderful time between the rain of rocks and fire and the loss of my village," Parner retorted, rolling his eyes.

"I found Pirulo in an oasis in the desert!" Aten defended. "Does the map have any oasis on it?"

"No!" Parner announced. "And we cannot see the most southern point of the desert on the map! Perhaps it is even lower than we can see!"

"How do you intend to lead us into a desert this size on your search for this mysterious oasis that you found... with your eyes closed!?" Trise yelled.

"I found him before; I can find him again," Aten said confidently.

"But how?" Ren asked.

"We must go into the desert in order to find—"

"Aten, this is a desert," Trise said. "Are you such a fool to believe we can enter without a plan. It is the Deserted Desert. There will be nothing there to help us!"

"When we first fled the dragon, you told us you knew how to find the bard... But your plan was to close your eyes and stumble through sand!?" Parner said, his fingers pinching the bridge of his nose.

"I recall you telling me that you were on the brink of death when you first found the bard. Do you intend to lead us to our deaths?" Trise asked sincerely.

Aten felt every wave of frustration that he had felt on this journey well up at once, and he gripped the table tightly.

"You do not have to come with me, I can go find Pirulo alone!" he screamed.

"Hey!" Top was suddenly behind him, placing a firm hand on Aten's shoulder. "Do not yell at the cripple! You are all upsetting him!"

Aten stood up suddenly, shoving his chair into the innkeeper.

"Nothing they have said upsets me more than you constantly referring to me as a 'cripple,' you halfwit," Aten responded, making his way back to his room.

"Just like I told you. You upset the cripple," Top said quietly, looking irritated at Aten's companions.

Aten slammed the door to the room and began packing food, his belongings, and dressing into his armor. He was furious with himself for how he yelled at his companions, but was also enraged at Top for being an annoying fool. He threw a few day's rations into a pack and hoisted it over his shoulder. He realized it was over his bad shoulder, but did not crumble under the pain. He had healed greatly. He attempted to raise the arm over his head, but it stuck around the level of his ear. It seemed his left arm would be permanently damaged. He shook his head, further frustrated.

The door opened as he was placing his sheathed sword around his waist, his four companions looking in from the hallway cautiously.

"Do you always walk away from conversations you are uncomfortable having?" Parner joked, stepping inside and sitting in front of Aten on his bed.

Aten thought back to Vesta once more. He had left her on more than one occasion because he was upset with something she had said. He shook her away from his thoughts.

All things led back to Vesta.

"This is not the first time I have left a conversation I thought was not worth my time," Aten admitted.

"Not worth your time," Trise said, disappointed.

"It is not," Aten nodded. "Not because you do not bring up valid arguments, but because I will venture into the desert regardless of the answer to your questions. I am grateful you came with me this far, but it seems I am to go alone from here."

Parner began chuckling.

"What?" Aten snapped.

"You speak as though I am not coming with you despite your recklessness," Parner laughed.

"What?" Aten repeated, this time confused.

"I told you I would follow you even if it came to my death," Ren said. "And though I am scared, I am also not going to leave my leader behind."

"But I…" Aten looked between them. "I do not know where I am going!"

"I knew that from the beginning," Trise nodded. "You wanted to come to Sekoa through rapids. I knew this was a fool's errand, but I am here to be a fool into the desert. We only wished to develop a plan before entering, but if you have decided to go in blind, then I suppose I have no choice."

Aten fell back on his bed overwhelmed. After all the anguish of his travels, he did not expect this response from those that brought him this far. He thought they would be tired of the endless chase and the perils of each and every land. Within each of them, he saw Roth's sincerity. A friend who he missed so much.

"You are our leader, yes. But you are also our friend. We will not leave you alone," Gertrude spoke.

Aten felt something come over him that he had not felt for a long time. Since the loss of his village, he felt hollow, angry, and frustrated at how the world treated him. But now he was overcome with emotion he had not felt since he had last seen Roth in

Vesta's cave. He had his fellow knights as well as archers whom he had once hated promising to follow him to the edges of the Deserted Desert. Aten began to cry tears of gratitude.

30

Aten stood at the edge of the desert, the cliff leading up to Sekoa behind them. They had thanked Fera and Top for their hospitality, snuck between the houses of Sekoa as stealthily as they could, and had reached the desert by the time the sun had peaked in the sky. The heat was as oppressive as it was overwhelming, baking every inch of skin not covered by cloth or armor.

"The Deserted Desert," Ren sighed, covering his face with his hand to shield his eyes from the sun's rays. "I feel that it may have been more wise to enter and travel at night than in the middle of the day."

"That may have been something to mention before we climbed down the face of a cliff," Parner sighed at him, readjusting the pack of food he had slung over his back.

"As if you could stop Aten if you tried," Trise said, dropping behind him. "He was adamant that he would leave immediately."

"I think the sun is nice. It will be good to darken my skin," Gertrude said.

"Thank you, Gertrude," Aten nodded to her. "The sun could do us well."

"Oh yes," Parner agreed sarcastically, looking to Trise, "it could remind us of the flames of Apophis."

"Keep us vigilant to his incinerating wrath!" Trise replied, smiling at Parner.

"Which way, Aten?" Roth asked, looking back up the sheer face of the cliff and taking a moment to decide whether he regretted everything he had done to get here.

"I do not know," Aten said, closing his eyes and beginning the trek into the desert.

"Dear God, he is really walking in blind," Parner groaned.

"I knew he did not speak of the way to find him in jest, but I still did not expect him to begin with it," Ren agreed.

The group walked miserably behind Aten, the sand holding them back significantly when the weight of their packs drove them deep into the ground with every step. Aten was unperturbed by every moan, groan, and comment from Parner as the sun lowered itself across the sky, pelting them with its harsh desert rays. Aten would stumble often, the acclivities of the desert dunes often catching him off guard with his eyes closed. He picked himself up, grateful for the returned strength in his limbs being able to withstand the strain.

Aten knew there were hundreds of miles of desert, but he was also determined to comb the entirety of it if it meant finding Pirulo. The bard would be the key. They were so close now. It would be just like when he met him after Vesta. He knew exactly how to defeat her, and this time he would not hesitate.

Even within the desert, all things led back to Vesta.

"Aten," Gertrude wheezed. "May we rest?"

Aten opened his eyes in surprise, only to close them when met with the blinding blaze of the desert sun. He opened them more slowly and turned around. Each of his companions were breathing heavily, drenched in their own sweat. Aten looked down at his own garments and saw they were equally weighed down by his perspiration. He had never expected Gertrude to ask for them to slow down, but it made sense if she was speaking on behalf of the good of the travelers as a whole.

"Very well," Aten nodded, only now realizing that he too was out of breath. How long had they been travelling? It must have been less than an hour, but it felt like a full day's worth of energy had seeped out of him.

Parner collapsed backward into the sand, pulling the food sack over his shoulder to pull pieces of food from within. Ren, Trise and Gertrude crowded around him. Aten came last as he distributed dried meat.

"Eat sparingly," Parner suggested.

N. T. Lazer

"Are we running low on food?" Trise asked, disappointed.

"No, but…" Parner hesitated and looked up at Aten. "I fear we may be in this desert for a long while."

Aten did not know how to respond. He did not expect to be out here for so long. The bard's song should have found him by now. Perhaps it was less mystical that he thought it to be. Perhaps it was nothing more than a suggestion, given that sound would travel better over mounds of the desert dunes.

After consuming their rations of food, the four looked up expectantly, yet apprehensively, to Aten. He could see the exhaustion in their eyes. The last thing he wanted to do was to force them to travel when they were at their limit.

"We should rest," Aten suggested.

"Thank God," Parner grumbled, laying his head flat on the sand and moving the food sack in the way of the sun to grant him a small haven of shade. Trise looked out at the desert, detesting it, while Gertrude looked through supplies to create shade for herself and the others.

"Ren," Aten said, "We need a plan."

"We needed a plan," Parner rolled over in place, wiping his forehead of sweat, "now we need a few graves."

"Shut up, Parner," Aten told him. "I did not expect we would be here for this long. It was so simple to find him on my last visit through the desert."

"*Visit,* he says," Parner laughed with a hint of delirium, "As though he commonly makes the trip to join Pirulo for a warm meal now and again."

"I am afraid Parner may be right," Ren said, approaching Aten. "We needed a plan before we entered. Now we are far into this burning land. The only reason I know the way back is because I know we need to head North to escape from here."

"Yes, but given that I am a fool and entered here without a plan, what is the next best thing?" Aten asked. The frustration he thought he had long buried returned to him. He had placed so much faith in reaching the desert that he did not consider the consequences of entering beyond the final moment of finding Pirulo. What once he considered the ultimate goal of his leadership now became a trial in itself.

Ren squatted down with his eyes closed. Aten stepped in the way of the sun to shade him while he thought. Ren opened his eyes, a look of uncertainty across them.

"We could travel at night?" he suggested.

"Then we would not be able to see," Trise shook her head.

"Aten has been walking with his eyes closed. It does not seem like much of a difference," Gertrude shrugged.

"Ah, but the difference would be that the sun would be down! That's brilliant Ren!" Parner smiled, raising an arm in the air in support.

"Yes," Aten nodded, considering the idea. "We travel by night and rest by day. We could begin to make camp at first light."

"Which means we are on the later end of my resting time!" Parner said.

"Bring out the cloth we brought as blankets. We can set them up with our sheaths and swords to block out the sun's light while we rest," Aten offered.

"Yes," Ren said, pulling the pack off his back and pulling out a few pieces of cloth. Together Aten and Ren set up makeshift tents and Trise, Gertrude and Parner crawled behind them.

Aten lay his head down on the sand, then sat up when he realized how hot the sand still was. He placed another cloth on the ground, laid down, and fell asleep.

31

The group of travelers trudged through their second night of the desert journey, their tire never fading even with sleep, but much more satisfied with the lack of burns and aches caused by the sun. They drank their water miserly, but with every sip came the reminder that it was a finite resource. Aten's eyes were closed, unable to take in the glittering expanse of stars above them. Gertrude would often look upward and nod to herself, assuring herself of something.

"First light!" Parner cried, pointing to the horizon. Aten opened his eyes to see the tiniest hint of an orange-red sheen stretch across the sky to the east. It was as beautiful as it was disappointing. They would begin to make camp. How long would it take to find Pirulo?

Aten dropped the bag on his back and pulled out his various articles of cloth to build a tent for Gertrude first then himself. He watched as she drew something into the sand with an arrow, looking up to the sky occasionally.

"What are you making?" Aten asked.

"It is Orion, the hunter," Gertrude answered.

"With dots in the sand?"

"Orion is a constellation, a collection of stars in the sky. It resembles an archer with a bow. I was to be named Orion if I was born a boy," Gertrude replied.

Aten looked up to the sky, its wide array of stars fading with the rising sun, then out to the horizon.

"I cannot see anything that resembles… well, anything," Aten admitted.

"The stars do not quite draw in straight lines, but rather are simply seated close enough together to have a resemblance to creatures," Gertrude pointed to the sky. Aten followed her direction and saw nothing significant.

"How did you learn so much about stars?" Aten asked.

"I used to guide us in the night on our raids and ambushes in Banti."

"I thought Trise led you all?"

"Trise led us to battle, but I led us to position. It is a very powerful ability to know the direction you are going when your enemies are blind to such means."

Aten thought about it for a moment, considering how valuable such a skill could be.

"Who taught you this ability of… star navigation?" Aten asked, planting the first piece of cloth firmly into the sand.

"Celestial navigation," Gertrude corrected, her eyes on the floor as she thought back, "was taught to me by my father."

"And where is he now?"

"Likely among the dead that populate Vesta's cave. He never cared much for me beyond teaching me how to use a bow and arrow and how to navigate the night. In fact, he had planned to leave me and join the Royal Guard of the North when he returned from his battle with Vesta. He always said he wanted to be put to rest among such brave knights. I suppose he got his wish," Gertrude said forlornly.

Aten thought about it for a moment.

"I believe my father may be with yours," Aten said aloud as he came to the realization.

"What are we talking about that is so imperative that it prevents my sleeping?" Parner asked, approaching the two of them.

"What happened to our fathers. Were they all killed by Vesta?" Aten asked him.

"Oh yes. Yours when you were just born, if I recall correctly. Ren and my own just as we were entering the guild, in hopes to follow their footsteps of becoming knights who were to face a dragon," Parner nodded.

"So then all of us have been brought together, not just by the cruelty of Apophis, but of the murders of his daughter," Gertrude said, surprised.

"It does not matter what killed them," Trise approached. "It matters that we kill Apophis. We cannot dwell on the past that we share."

"But Trise," Gertrude protested, "if we do not learn history, we could miss crucial information that could benefit us all. How did we learn to use the bow except by learning from years of perfecting the craft by those that studied before them?"

"Very well, history is important, but could you put it to use and became more adept with your bow? No, that requires you to be here in the present," Trise reminded her. "And I wish to presently rest. I am weary."

"And we shall spar," Aten pointed to Ren who turned around and widened his eyes when he realized he was being pointed at.

"Again? We sparred yesterday morning?"

"And you have yet to best me. Hurry now, we will use our sheaths," Aten picked up his sword sheath and left his sword in the sand. Ren reluctantly did the same. Trise, Gertrude and Parner watched from their shaded spaces.

Aten began relentlessly attacking, forcing Ren to react faster than he could think. Ren had a difficult time going on the offensive, and Aten planned to beat that idea out of him. Aten had left the previous session with a rather low number of bruises. He wanted to break down whatever inhibitions Ren had. He disarmed him and put his sheath to Ren's neck.

"Faster, Ren!" he demanded, indicating for him to pick his sheath up again.

Aten swung his sheath down at Ren who swiped it away at the last moment.

"You are hesitating! There is not time for thought or fear!" Aten coached him, swinging again.

Aten and Ren had been sparring since setting up the tent at first light. They agreed that the only chance Ren could learn to face an enemy is if he was at the very least comfortable beating Aten at a sparring session. Thus far, Aten bested him every time.

"You are too aggressive!" Ren complained.

"I am aggressive because if I am not, my foe will kill me!" Aten replied, stabbing at him. Ren pulled his stomach back, narrowly avoiding it.

"Well done!" Parner cheered on, swinging his fists from behind his tent.

Aten thrust again, stabbing at Ren's hand and spinning his sheath, disarming the knight. Before he could deal a blow to his neck, Ren kicked up sand in Aten's eyes, blinding him. Aten swung twice blindly before Ren jumped behind him and pushed him down.

"I am sorry Aten, I did not—"

"Well fought Ren!" Aten said from the floor, "You just bested me in combat!" His eyes were closed but his teeth were beaming, magnified by the rising sun.

Trise and Gertrude applauded him politely while Parner screamed in jubilation, throwing handfuls of sand in the air in celebration. Ren smiled bashfully, hardly believing he was able to defeat Aten.

"I think this calls for a celebration in the form of sleep!" Parner said confidently, laying his head down in the shade of his cloth and closing his eyes.

"Aten," Ren put his hand on Aten's shoulder as he stood up and cleaned his eyes.

"There is no need to apologize, Ren. I hope you would do the same in a real battle," Aten assured him.

"No, it is not that," he said, his voice level and quiet. "We need to consider how long we have been out in the desert. It has been two full days. We are running low on food, energy, and most importantly water. We need to leave the desert."

Aten felt at the waterskin he had tied to his waist. He had already finished the contents of his first and wanted nothing more than to down the remainder of the second. But he needed it to last.

"Not to worry, Ren. There is more water at Pirulo's oasis," Aten said confidently.

"I am worried we will not find the oasis," Ren told him sincerely.

"I am confident we will."

"Your confidence is not enough to keep us alive! We need to find water or we will all perish. The strength of your will cannot outdo the needs of your body. You will march to your death with your eyes closed," Ren insisted.

Aten blinked and looked down to the sandy ground.

"We must leave," Ren repeated.

"No… No!" Aten persisted. "We did not come this far only to retreat! He is right across the next dune! Pirulo is here!"

"You have gone hours with your eyes closed and nothing to show for it. It may be time to admit that finding the bard was just something that came with being near to Pallas. We can start from Pallas and search once more after we replenish our supplies."

"No!" Aten said, his hands running through his hair. He had brought them all this far. To leave now would be to admit defeat. He had to find Pirulo. He needed to listen closer to the sounds of the desert. "We cannot defeat Apophis unless we have Pirulo! We have to find—"

"You do not know that!" Ren's grip tightened on Aten's shoulder. "We do not know Pirulo will have anything to say that will be helpful—"

"I do! I am sure of it! He will tell us the secret to defeat the dragon and we will save Kolog!"

"No! He will likely tell us to strike at its heart, just as he did about Vesta! What is so special about this dragon that will cause Pirulo to act any different—"

Aten kicked at sand in frustration and something flew out, smacking Ren in the shin. Ren knelt down quickly.

"Ouch!"

"I apologize! What was it that hit you?" Aten asked, his frustration taking a moment to rest as his worry took hold.

"It was a…" Ren stared at a rock he picked up from the sand. He rolled it around in his fingers, its makeup a strange swirl of combined textures, as if lightning had frozen into sand.

"What is that?" Aten asked.

"I do not know," Ren said, digging further into the sand they squatted above. Ren pulled out a larger rock of the same makeup. It resembled an explosion, but caught in an envelope of sand.

"I have never seen such a rock before. Are these common in the desert?" Aten asked.

"This… I have read about this once before. It was said to have been found by our ancestors on the outskirts of Pallas at the entrance to the desert after a lightning storm. It is fulgurite," Ren looked at the larger rock, fascinated.

"It just appeared?" Aten asked.

"It is the result of increasing the temperature of sand with immense heat, like a blast of lightning."

"Or…" Aten swallowed. "Or a dragon's flame?"

Ren looked up quickly and thought. He nodded slightly.

Aten thrust himself up and climbed the nearest dune in haste. Ren came after him, unsure what Aten was looking for but curious all the same. When Aten reached the top, he gasped, his eyes overwhelmed. Ren followed close behind and gasped as well, looking out in a horrified awe.

In front of them sat a sea of fulgurite of all shapes leading in the same direction as if a paintbrush slid across the desert and left rocks in its wake. Aten could not believe the quantity of rocks before him, spreading as far as he could see, but was further distraught to see where the path of rocks ended. An oasis.

"Wake up!" Aten screamed to those below. "Everyone wake up, we found Pirulo!"

Aten ran ahead while Ren went back to help the others pack and prepare to move to the oasis. Aten jumped between the fulgurite, taking note of the fact that even the ground he walked on was more stable than all the sand he had crossed, as if it was paved with gravel. As the oasis grew nearer, Aten's worries grew more serious. The trees that had been covering the water were scorched, though still standing. The spring was still as inviting as it was the last time he saw it, if not more, but he did not see the makings of an unlit campfire under the trees where Pirulo sat previously.

N. T. Lazer

Aten ran faster, willing himself to overcome all of his travel's fatigue so he could finally make it to the coveted destination. He finally approached the oasis itself and thought he could see the charred remains to a campfire. When he scrutinized it a moment longer he saw that it was the remains of Pirulo's lute.

"No," Aten said quietly, then looked up further. "NO!"

Laying a few paces away, with a charred hand outstretched to the scorched lute were the black, burnt remains of Pirulo, the bard of old.

32

Parner was the first to arrive at the oasis, running in and shoving his face into the spring as soon as he arrived. He drank excessively, then threw his head back and exhaled, satisfied.

"I must say Aten, when you woke me from atop the dune, I did not expect to be presented with such a pleasant—Dear Lord!" Parner retreated a step when he saw Aten kneeling above Pirulo's dead body. "Is that him?"

Aten nodded sharply, dejected.

"This is the oasis?" Gertrude asked with wonder as she entered the area. "It is quite… Oh no… Oh Aten."

The rest of Aten's companions gathered behind him, looking at Pirulo's body. Aten's entire body felt tight, every muscle strained against itself. Pirulo was dead. He had traveled half the kingdom and put his friends in constant danger. And Pirulo was dead. He trembled in rage, frustration, and confusion.

"Apophis burned it down. He killed Pirulo," Aten hissed, his eyes screwed shut.

"So it seems," Ren nodded, looking around the remains of Pirulo's belongings.

"We are lost… We are done," Aten stammered. "I am sorry. I am so sorry. There is nothing that can stop Apophis. I should have gone to

Kolog myself and let myself be slain by Apophis long ago."

"No, Aten, we must think. There must be another—"

"Another what, Ren? A plan? What is the plan, then? What can be done? The dragon is faster than anything that exists in this world, more powerful than any weapon we hold, and now has more control of the kingdom than any of us! What would you have us do? What is your plan!" Aten screamed.

Ren looked back at the others who stared, stunned. Parner stepped forward and spoke carefully,

"It is not as bad as it seem—"

"Shut up Parner! Shut up! I begged you all to risk your lives for nothing! Pallas is gone, and any village could be next! It… It…" Aten fell on his back and stared up, despondent.

"Aten," Ren called him.

Aten did not respond, his eyes dry and his breathing labored.

"What are we to do now?" Gertrude asked, worried. "I thought Pirulo would have the answers we seeked to defeat this thing."

"We should practice our archery," Trise determined.

"Do not jest," Gertrude replied.

"I am not. If we are to face the dragon with no additional information, we must be experts at our crafts. Come, Gertrude, we will use the base of this tree as the target. Let the knights bring Aten back from where his mind has gone."

"What about P—what about the body?" Gertrude asked.

"You are right. The man deserves a burial," Trise agreed.

The two archers picked up Pirulo's burned body and lute and went off to the other side of the spring to dig him a resting place.

"They intend to give us space to talk to him," Ren told Parner.

"Aten, get up," Parner said, walking up to the knight and putting an arm out to help him stand up. Aten's eyes remained looking past Parner, his face not even registering his words. "Ren, what do we do?"

"Sometimes it is best to take a break and allow someone to calm down on their own accord. Do not aggravate him further. Let him experience all of these feelings and talk to us when he is ready," Ren said, sitting next to Aten patiently.

Parner looked between the two of them.

"That sounds foolish or boring; I am not sure which one exactly. I will make us some food since it seems we are staying here for a short while," Parner decided, taking off his pack of food and rummaging through it to grab material.

Aten breathed deeply, his limbs shaking with a concoction of emotions he could not even begin to describe. Were those that died at Berdun on his account? If he had simply gone to Apophis when still in Pallas, would they live to this day? Would the King of Kolog still be in power? Would Pallas still be in one piece? What if he had never killed Vesta? None of this would have happened. Even Pirulo would still be alive.

All things led back to Vesta.

He cursed himself for running his fellow knights and archers on this fool's errand, even after being told many times that it may prove less than what he expected. He cursed his companions for not fighting him harder and allowing him to drag them this far. They all had new scars because of his negligence. But most of all he cursed Apophis. He hated that the beast existed and that there was nothing he could do about it. How could anyone strike at the monster's heart when he clearly killed everything in his sight? And Aten still did not know whether the strike to the heart was literal or metaphorical. Even a simple answer to that question would have made this trip worth it. But Pirulo was dead. And Aten had nothing to show for his journey. He clenched his fists tightly and smashed them against the floor, feeling like such a naive child. He had expected so much out of this encounter that he had not even considered that this could be a possibility.

His breathing had slowed down now. He did not know how long he had been lying on the floor, but the sun seemed to have risen considerably since he laid there. He picked his head and looked around slowly. Trise and Gertrude were sitting next to Parner, eating a small meal and helping themselves to the water from the spring. They seemed in good spirits considering the situation that Aten felt they were in. He looked up and saw that they were shaded and realized that even though the sun had risen, he felt no discomfort over his body. He looked around further and saw Ren sitting next to him, waiting patiently. Ren smiled.

"Do you wish to speak?" Ren asked, amiably.

"I failed," Aten said finally.

"I do not know what you took the time to think about, but I thought about why Pirulo would be dead," Ren said, ignoring Aten's self-condemnation.

"Why? Because Apophis killed him!"

"Yes, but why? Why would Apophis kill him?"

"Because he is a mad dragon who destroys the kingdom as he sees fit."

"No, Aten! Think! Why would Apophis come to the desert? At first glance there would be nothing out here!" Ren pressed.

"Per... Perhaps Apophis knew of Pirulo?"

"Right! And if he knew about Pirulo, then why would he come out into the desert to find him? Why kill him? He is just one man!"

"It could be… Perhaps…" Aten could not piece together an answer. "I do not know."

"Because you were right, Aten! Because Pirulo knew something about how to defeat a dragon and Apophis wished to scrub that knowledge from the world! Did you see the state of Pirulo's remains? It was incredibly old. Apophis must have come here days ago, perhaps even before he arrived at Pallas! I believe the bard was his first victim," Ren said.

Aten blinked, surprised. It elated him slightly to know that there may have been reason to come here after all. But he did not feel much better overall.

"But he is dead now, so whatever knowledge he had has died with him," Aten responded.

"No, there must be more to this. Bards did not learn except from existing stories and history. There must be some form of information out there, whether in a bard's song or a merchant's gossip. You were right Aten, there is something more!" Ren repeated.

Aten took the words to heart, but was not convinced. He had placed so much hope into Pirulo, he did not want to rush into placing more hope in another false lead. They traveled the desert to learn there was information that used to be here and was now burned. He shook his head.

Aten stood with Ren's help and made his way to Parner, Trise, and Gertrude to eat with them.

"Finished your tantrum?" Trise asked, looking up to Aten.

"It seems Parner is not the only one I should be asking to shut up," Aten said, sitting down next to Parner. Parner smiled between the two of them, handing Aten some fish.

"Good to see your wits are back," Parner said.

"I still feel awful," Aten admitted.

"Well, there will be plenty of time for that while we make our way out of the desert and… Where are we going?" Parner asked him.

"Are there any villages or cities nearby?" Aten asked, looking out across the sand. He remembered how to get back to Pallas from here, having been instructed by Pirulo the last time he visited.

"I do not know where we are," Ren said, dropping the map in front of Aten. He looked at it between bites of fish and pointed to a town at the southern edge of the Western Range.

"Merdo?" he asked. "I am unfamiliar with this place."

"It is a city that merchants use to travel between Kolog and the western Kingdom of Mimi," Parner answered, pointing to a space to the left of the map.

"This is where we should go. I can lead us to this southern edge of Vesta Forest. It would be good for us to rest in a bed before marching to my death," Aten decided.

"Beg your pardon?" Gertrude asked, worried.

"I will turn myself in to Kolog after escorting you out of here. I hope that Apophis will go back to the pit he appeared from if I am only to be killed by his hand," Aten explained.

"We cannot let you do that," Parner said.

"You know well that you will not be able to stop me given enough time. And in the case that my death does not drive Apophis away, then perhaps you can find a way to defeat him with Ren's help," Aten suggested.

"What does he mean, Ren?" Trise asked.

"I thought that if Apophis came to this specific location to find this specific bard, then there must have been some information that Apophis did not want the world to have. And bards got their songs from history. So, the history must exist somewhere."

"So there is still a chance!" Gertrude said, excited.

"For you, yes. But I will turn myself in, regardless. Perhaps we do not need to find this secret in order to get him to leave this land," Aten said, determined.

"Well, I will follow you to your death, then," Parner said, smiling.

"Parner, do not joke," Aten said sternly.

"I am not," Parner shook his head.

Aten looked between the others sitting with him and realized they would follow him as well. His anger and frustration subsided for a short moment, but remained the most powerful emotion in him, raging at his ignorance and foolishness to drag such good people through the desert.

"You are all too stubborn," Aten shook his head.

"We learned from our leader," Parner smiled.

33

Aten took his first few steps into Vesta Forest, free from the sand of the desert. He was still sour, a pit of anger hanging slightly into his stomach. The forest was only a faint memory of what it used to be. While the trees nearest to them stood tall, the rest of the forest was ash and petrified wood. Parner looked around him, happy to finally be on solid ground instead of the loose piles of sand he dragged himself through.

"I had considered hunting for food when we entered the forest. I had not considered it would be…" Parner let his silence complete the sentence. There was no life within the heart of the forest. Only destruction and the reminders of Apophis's rage.

"Parner," Trise said quietly, a hint of alarm in her voice.

Aten turned and saw her wielding her bow, an arrow already nocked in place. Gertrude had done the same. They watched the trees closely. Aten unsheathed his blade immediately and held it up tensely.

"What is it?" Aten asked her.

"We are being watched. Two behind the tree to the north of us and four behind trees just behind it," Trise answered.

"I see five more to the tree a few dozen paces to the west of that," Gertrude added.

"You are perceptive, I will give you that," someone said from behind a tree, stepping out with his hands up. His hands were red, scarred from burns.

"It is the man Top described from Sekoa," Gertrude whispered.

"How did they follow us here?" Aten asked.

"I knew we would find you here. Children cannot help but run home when they are out of options. Welcome home to Pallas. I am sure everyone here will be delighted to see you," the man said. A few others came out from behind trees, armed with swords and bows alike. There were eleven total.

"Here on Captain Torbough's orders?" Aten asked, gripping his sword tightly.

"Torbough? No, not on his word. We are here on our own accord! I am Olan. And I, along with my crew, am going to be the richest man in Kolog when I bring you to King Apophis," Olan said, wiggling his burned fingers in anticipation.

"Have you not heard? The king is a dragon. He burned down Pallas and B—"

"I know that! How do you think I got these hands!" Olan spat. "He did not take kindly to hearing that we lit the signal flame only to announce you had escaped! Nevertheless, it is no business of mine what manner of beast the King is, only that he pays handsomely."

Aten eyes went wide with rage. His fists shook wildly and his teeth grit firmly together.

"You work for the dragon willingly?" Aten screamed.

"We do, for he is—"

Aten took the time to address his comrades.

"How many archers are there? Can you successfully take them out first?" he whispered Trise and Gertrude.

"There are four of them. We can strike them quickly, but there is no telling what damage they can do in the time it takes for us to nock an arrow between our releasing shafts," Trise answered quietly.

"Parner, Ren, are you ready?" Aten asked.

"If I must," Parner answered sincerely.

"Aten, they are not fighters," Ren said, his voice quivering. "They are laymen in search of riches. Speak to them and calm them down. We do not have to fight."

Aten took an instant to glance at him and saw him shivering in place.

"Ren, please, get behind a tree. Something to protect yourself from potential incoming arrows."

Ren did not respond. Aten refused to allow these men free when they knowingly worked for the dragon. The one that had caused all this anger and rage to swirl within him. He would let out the rage among his followers.

"—not as if the previous king, Faro, was any more altruistic than Apophis! *He* never gave us an opportunity to come upon such riches!" Olan completed his thought.

"And if I come peacefully?" Aten asked. He shifted the weight of his sack and indicated it to Parner. Parner understood immediately, nodding his head.

"Aten… please," Ren made one last plea.

"Then I suppose we tie up your friends and leave them to die," Olan shrugged, "We cannot have them come after you when they are out of—"

"Now!" Aten screamed, "Kill all in the forest!" Aten spun once and placed his sack of food between himself and his enemies.

Many things happened simultaneously. Parner threw his sack of food just as had been done to him on the river between Dervin and Sekoa and a rain of food fell upon the opposing archers, pelting them and causing some to lose their focus. Trise and Gertrude launched arrows at the enemy archers, catching one in the neck and the other in the eye. Trise screamed and two more arrows came flying at Aten. He ducked under one and caught the other with his sack before throwing it at the remaining archers.

"It snapped!" Aten heard Trise scream from behind him. He also heard a scream emitted from Parner followed by something falling to the ground.

Aten closed the gap between himself and Olan within a moment and drove his sword at his heart. Olan just barely moved to one side and Aten kicked dirt into his eyes as he had seen Ren do the night before, blinding him and stabbing into his heart, this time making contact. Olan let out a short, staccato cry before crumpling, lifeless. Aten's eyes were engulfed in rage and he ran upon the next man who had held his arms up in fear after seeing how quickly Aten overcame their leader.

Aten heard someone call out from behind him, but he killed the man in front of him, ignoring his pleas. It was exhilarating. Aten looked around, his eyes feral now, and saw two archers on the ground, dead, and the remaining raiders running in fear. Aten began to chase after them before something grabbed him from behind. He wheeled around and began swinging his sword, but whoever held onto him pushed down painfully on his wounded shoulder, causing him to drop the arm wielding his sword. When he fully turned, he saw that Parner stood before him, hanging on with one arm, the other soaked in blood.

"Stop Aten!" Parner screamed at his face.

"No! But the—the others they will—"

"Aten, the battle is won! Are you so weak in constitution that you would drown in bloodlust at the first death by your hand?" Parner shoved Aten away forcefully.

Aten looked back at the fleeing attackers. They were long gone, scampering as fast as their legs could carry them. He now noticed how rigidly he gripped his blade and how powerful his breaths were. Aten looked back at his companions. Trise was consoling Gertrude, apologizing for something. Ren stood shaking in place. And Parner had an arrow sticking through his arm. All the remaining rage in Aten drained away.

"What happened?" Aten asked, shocked.

"Aten, do not look at me, look around. Acknowledge the death you brought upon these men, then we can talk about me. That man surrendered and you cut him down. Look at him and convince yourself he deserved it," Parner ordered.

Aten looked at the two men he had killed. The first time he had taken the life of a fellow man. Two, one after another, as if the first did not matter enough to stop another from dying. He looked at Olan for a long while. The man had been speaking only moments before, now never again.

"He had to die. His greed was so powerful that he served Apophis," Aten gestured to Olan.

"I agree," Parner nodded. "I do not think he would have left me alive if you had gone peacefully, rather he would have killed us to make sure his trail was not followed. And that man?" Parner gestured to the other.

Aten had not even realized the other man had surrendered. He was overtaken by the battle. He had never done anything so extreme as to kill someone, but all of his sparring made it come naturally.

"He… he was among those that sought greed over anything. This seems to be a fitting end for him. He was a coward, too," Aten determined.

"A coward? Does that mean Ren deserves to die?" Parner asked.

"No! Of course n—I see what you are saying. No, he did not deserve to die for being a coward, but for being among those that served the dragon," Aten said.

"Very well," Parner said, wincing as pain in his arm flared. "I wanted to ensure that you were thinking rationally before we continued. I do not agree that the man who surrendered deserved to die here, but considering he was willing to kill me for some gold, I am not very upset at the outcome," Parner shrugged, smiling weakly.

Aten looked down at Parner's bleeding arm and back to the two men he killed.

"I… I am sorry Parner. I do not know why I acted this way. I became a monster," Aten said remorsefully.

"That you did, similar to the one that used to live here."

Aten realized that he had told his companions to 'Kill all in the forest,' similar to what he recalled

Vesta to have said when she killed the Royal Guard of the North in the terrible massacre outside of her cave.

"What happened?" Aten asked, now much more calm, though his heart still pumped chaotically in his chest.

"Oh my God!" Trise approached them stunned, looking at the blood spilling from Parner. There was a long, red line across her face that made way for a thin stream of blood. "What happened?" she asked.

"I was hit with an arrow when I tried to stop it from hitting Ren," Parner said. "But do not worry! The pain from it exceeds the worst pain I have ever felt before in my life!"

"That sounds awful!" Trise said, worried.

"Oh, much worse than that," Parner nodded.

"Let me try to clean the wound and perhaps cover it properly," Trise said.

"You know how to do that?"

"Gertrude and I know many ways of healing someone hit with an arrow," she replied, leading him back to one of the sacks now on the floor.

"What happened to your face?" Aten asked, following them.

"We overused our bows in practice. I slipped applying the arrow and my bow dry fired and snapped. This is what happens when all the tension in your string goes to your face instead of your bow," Trise answered.

Aten stood in front of the petrified Ren and snapped his fingers.

"You sh-should not h-have fought them," Ren stuttered.

"Perhaps you could have talked to them, as we both know it is not my strong point," Aten answered.

Ren looked down, ashamed.

"It seems Parner took an arrow for you in his left arm," Aten said.

"I am sorry," Ren muttered, somehow even further ashamed.

"We will get better," Aten promised him. "You and I alike have much to learn when it comes to fighting."

Ren nodded, determined and went to check on Gertrude. Aten returned to Parner and Trise to see her applying a bandage. Parner was somehow laughing, even now.

"It seems the arrow severed some nerves," Trise told Aten, she was wiping the blood off her face now. "He cannot move his fingers."

"Look Aten! Perhaps Top will call us the Cripple Brothers now!" Parner pointed to his left hand with his right. Aten smirked despite himself.

"I am glad you are in high spirits," Aten nodded.

"I am! For I learned you are not actually willing to give yourself to Apophis. Otherwise, you may have considered Olan's offer before killing him," Parner smiled.

Aten blinked, surprised.

"I suppose I needed to be reminded of the evils of Apophis. He cannot have me without a fight," Aten promised.

"Excellent," Parner nodded. "I would offer you my hand in support, but it seems to be in excruciating pain."

"Shut up, Parner," Aten said, looking West to find a path to Merdo.

34

"Perhaps we should be proactive," Aten said, standing suddenly at the inn, surrounded by the hustle and bustle of merchants inside.

They had been waiting patiently for food to be served to them, finally resting their legs after days of travel. Aten looked between Trise and Parner, Trise with a fresh scar on her face from her bowstring and Parner who could not move fingers aside from his thumb and forefinger on his left hand. They laughed at a joke between themselves, and Aten found it both reassuring and interesting how carefree they acted given their situation. Ren raised a knowing eyebrow to Parner then turned to address Aten.

"What do you mean?" Ren asked, recoiling at the idea of expending more energy when still exhausted by the journey.

"We should ask all of the merchants whether they know anything about how to defeat Apophis," Aten said, leaving the table. He looked around and was surprised to see how many merchants were among them in the inn. Evidently, they came to a popular location.

"Wait, Roth! What if they recognize you?" Ren said quietly.

"Then they will have excellent gossip to deliver to the Kingdom of Mimi," Aten said nonchalantly, walking to the table neighboring them.

"—heard it from Marc and his daughter Didra—"

"Excuse me," Aten interrupted a conversation. "What do you know of dragons?"

"I know that one has been killed recently in the forest not far from here, what do you know of dragons, boy?" one of the two men at the table responded, his beard was a clean sheen of brown and his eyes were hungry for information.

"I know," Aten lowered his voice, "That one has claimed the throne of Kolog."

The merchants at the table looked to one another with fascination.

"Apophis?" the other, a bald man, asked.

"A dragon?" the bearded one said.

"Aye," Aten nodded. "Do you know anything of dragon weaknesses?" he continued.

"Nothing much. There are the dragon wars of old, but nothing recent," the bald one shrugged. The other nodded.

"Thank you for the information," Aten rolled two bronze coins on the table.

"Ha!" the man with the beard guffawed, "Is this your first time conversing with merchants, boy?"

"I… well not quite my first, but—"

"We pay one another with information, not coin," the bald one said helpfully.

"Oh, ummm…" Aten scratched the back of his neck, unsure of what else he had to offer.

"You already paid, boy! We were not aware the king is the dragon!" the hairy one slapped the coins on the table, sliding them back to Aten.

"Indeed, and it makes the rumors surrounding the king make sense. I am sure it will be quite valuable to share in Mimi," the bald one nodded.

"Very well, thank you," Aten nodded, leaving the men be.

He went to the next table and asked them the same series of questions, with not much difference in answer. Not one of the merchants knew anything particularly insightful about how to defeat Apophis. Some mentioned Vesta, others brought up the burnt forest and villages, and a small number mentioned the wars of old. Aten returned to the table, while his companions' expectant pairs of eyes watched him.

"Nothing much," Aten shook his head.

"Well, what exactly did they have to share?" Ren asked.

"None of them were privy to the fact Apophis is a dragon," Aten began, "Most of them believed him a sorcerer, or just someone built on a throne of rumors. When asked of dragons, most reference Vesta and her nearby forest, and a handful mentioned dragon wars of old."

Trise shook her head.

"That is true, it is not much to go on," she said.

"A valiant effort," Parner nodded to Aten.

"Not much to go on?" Gertrude balked. "Did you pursue the information of the dragon wars any further?"

"We are not in need of dragon history," Aten said, confused.

"Dragon war!" Gertrude looked around the table, surprised that no one was picking up on her line of thinking. "As in battles with dragons that caused them to die!"

"We do not know that they died," Parner pointed out.

"Then why is it that Apophis is the first free-roaming dragon we have seen in generations? Vesta was believed to be the last, which is why Pallas threw so many of their men at her to defeat her," Gertrude argued.

"Yes, but that does not mean that—"

"Go ask them the nature of dragon wars, then we can continue this discussion," Ren suggested.

Aten got back up and went to the table next to him once more with the bald and bearded men.

"What do you know of the dragon war itself?" Aten asked.

"Not much. What do you know of what happened to Berdun?" the bald one asked. Aten understood that they were trading information once more.

"Apophis personally burned it down, including its inhabitants," Aten responded.

"Unreal," the bearded man whispered. "Any survivors?"

"Not that I know of," Aten replied. "And the dragon war?"

"Ancient history of the land that Torn and Kolog stand on. It was catalogued into a book: *The Dragon War*. The author may have been a little unimaginative with the name, but the information inside is supposedly sound. It is said that most dragons perished in those times, though the way they died has not been passed down. It may just be random acts of God for all we know," the bearded man explained.

"So if a dragon war was enough to wipe out the dragons, then there must be something that kills them. Something used to cause such massive destruction in the war!" Aten said, growing hopeful. Perhaps there still was a chance to defeat the new King of Kolog.

"Are there any copies of this book existing today?" Aten asked.

The bald one chuckled.

"What?" Aten asked.

"It exists, but no one from Kolog would be able to get their hands on it," he replied.

"Why not? Does it lie in the capital of Kolog along with the king?" Aten asked.

"No, much worse. It lies in the library catacombs under the capital of Torn," the bearded man told him. "You should know when to stop pursuing something that will kill you, boy," he warned.

"I know my limits," Aten agreed, thanking them for their time and information. He went back to his companions.

"It seems I will be traveling to Torn," Aten said immediately.

Trise and Gertrude looked to one another worried while Parner and Ren dropped their jaws.

"Well," Parner sighed, "can we at least skip the part where you try to convince us it is too dangerous to have us come along and we have to convince you that we will follow anyway?"

"I can allow that," Aten nodded, smiling.

"Very well, what is our destination in the wretched kingdom?"

"The capital city," Aten said grandly. "We will find the secret to the *Dragon War*."

AFTERWORD

Hello! I feel it is necessary to start off the Afterword with a shoutout to my Kickstarter backers. Whether you backed it or not, the reason this book is in your hands (or, ebook hands?) is as a result of their support. Thank you all immensely.

I added an Afterword at the end of *The Young Knight's Dragon Plight* and thought that would be it. I didn't want to be conceited and constantly adding chapters for self-aggrandizement, but it seems many of my fans reached out as a result of reading the Afterword, and appreciated the extra insight into the book. So, you all get another one!

Where in the first book, I knew that Vesta would die from the very beginning, the whole narrative around book two was one of obsession to find Pirulo. The scene I was building up to was Aten finding the bard in the oasis within the Deserted Desert and his subsequent catatonic state. Kind of a reflection on material pursuits in this life and what happens if you don't taper your obsessions. You could be rendered despondent over something that shouldn't have had that much control over you to begin with.

Much like the first book, I added things while on my way through that were not part of the initial plan. So here are some fun facts: I was actually going to kill off Parner right at Chapter 07! When I reached the scene where Apophis was supposed to end up killing him, I kind of had a liking to the character and thought "maybe it's a little soon for him to die off…" It also felt kind of "cheap" to do it then. Aten had just lost his village, now he was going to lose another member of his hometown? It wouldn't help with growth nor would it really have an impact on the reader. No one would have said "aw man, not Parner!" So I told myself I'd do it later, perhaps in Banti. But later never came. The more I told Parner to shut up, the more I wanted to write him dialogue. And now, he became a fun member of the main cast.

Ren has a copy of the map that the book uses! Anytime they're referring to the parchment of a map that Ren has with him, they're just looking at the same map that comes with this book. I always thought it would be neat to follow along a one-to-one copy of a fantasy novel's map.

When I outlined this book, I ended up with twenty chapters. Somehow that ballooned to thirty-four when I fit in the details I thought were necessary to add.

Lastly, I have notes on where Apophis was and what he was up to during the course of this book. Narratively, we follow Aten's point of view so there wasn't anywhere to really place it, but I might someday come around to writing the same story from

Apophis's and Vesta's point of view once the third book is out.

Thanks for reading, hope you enjoyed it! Feel free to reach out and give me feedback, always love to hear from my readers!

If you enjoyed **THE YOUNG KNIGHT AND THE OLD DRAGON,**
look out for

THE YOUNG KNIGHT AND THE DRAGON WAR

Book 3 of The Young Knight Series

by N. T. Lazer

Made in USA - Kendallville, IN
1233403_9781735561622
02.15.2021 1251